OTHER YEARLING BOOKS YOU WILL ENJOY:

Eyes in the Fishbowl

by Zilpha Keatley Snyder

Drawings by Alton Raible

A Yearling Book

Published by
Dell Publishing
a division of
The Bantam Doubleday Dell Publishing Group, Inc.
1 Dag Hammarskjold Plaza
New York, New York 10017

Yearling ® TM 913705, Dell Publishing,
a division of the Bantam Doubleday Dell Publishing Group, Inc.

ISBN: 0-440-40060-0

Reprinted by arrangement with Macmillan Publishing Company on
behalf of Atheneum Publishers

Printed in the United States of America

July 1988

10 9 8 7 6 5 4 3 2 1

CW

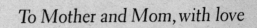

To Mother and Mom, with love

Eyes in the
Fishbowl

Chapter 1

LAST NIGHT I GOT THE IDEA TO PUT THE WHOLE THING into a song. I've been writing songs again lately, but this wasn't like the others. What I had in mind was a kind of ballad, a song story like the ancient troubadors used to make up about an important event so it would never be forgotten. I wrote the chorus first and it went like this——

The Fishbowl Song
by Dion James

Nobody's shopping at Alcott-Simpson's
The very best store in town.
Nobody's dropping by Alcott-Simpson's
Since the rumors started going around.
Strange things have been heard there,
And stranger things are seen,
And a customer fainted dead away—
In the French Room
On the Mezzanine.

3

I did that much in about fifteen minutes and it, like they say, almost wrote itself. I worked out a melody and some chords and it sounded so good that I would have called up Jerry or Brett to tell them about it right then except it was pretty late already, and a school day today.

So instead I started in on the first verse, but that's where I bogged down. It was hard to know where to start—what to put in and what to leave out. Obviously you couldn't put the whole thing into two or three verses. I started going over it, trying to get some ideas —and the first thing I knew I'd gone back to the very beginning.

The real beginning—at least for the store and the people in it—must have been a little less than a year ago, around the time I first saw Sara. But for me the beginning went back to a long time before that. In a way, my part in the whole thing started about six years ago on the day I first discovered Alcott-Simpson's. I was eight or nine years old at the time, and had just started to shine shoes on the corner of Palm and Eighth Avenue. Of course, it was only natural that it made a big impression on me when I first saw it. When I was eight years old—for various reasons having to do with my health and family situation—I'd hardly ever been outside my own neighborhood. Up until the day when José, who runs the flower stand on the corner of Palm and Eighth, found me being chased up an alley by some other shoeshine boys whose territory I'd wandered into, I'd never really been uptown; and my idea of a department store was Barney's Bargain Center two blocks from our house. But then José said I could set up shop right outside his flower stand where he could look out for me, so I went with him to Palm and Eighth and there it was—a whole block of marble pillars, crystal chandeliers and gilded wood. I mean, it was like I was Aladdin and the genii had just plopped me down in the middle of an enchanted palace.

I was only in the store a few minutes that first time, but I can still remember how it was. For one thing, it was right then, that first time, that I got that feeling of walking into a separate world. After the ordinary winter world outside, dirty gray with a cold wet wind, inside Alcott-Simpson's was like being on a different planet. The warmth was clean and smooth and loaded with something that was too high class to be called a smell. As a matter of fact, I was still standing just inside the door trying to sort out the smell—I'd gotten about as far as new cloth and leather and perfume and dollar bills—when somebody came along and invited me out. From then on, I was always prowling around Alcott-Simpson's—and being invited out from time to time.

My main enemy was Mr. Priestly, who was in charge of the store detectives. It's easy to see why he didn't appreciate me hanging around Alcott-Simpson's looking the way I used to until a couple of years ago.

If you can picture a bundle from the Good-Will's trash bin, with a mop of curly hair, a bad limp and dragging a big shoeshine kit, you'll know what I must have looked like. It couldn't have been good for the Alcott-Simpson image. But even after I changed a lot, and started dressing better, Priestly and his henchmen didn't much like having me around, because by then they were convinced that I was a shoplifter.

They were dead wrong about that, because I never took anything from Alcott-Simpson's that I didn't pay for. I'm not sure why exactly. It was no big moral thing with me, and I certainly had chances. Maybe it was just that I've never liked taking risks—or maybe it had something to do with the way I felt about the store. It would almost have been like stealing from myself. Anyway, I didn't. But Priestly was hard to convince, and two or three times he had me taken upstairs and searched. He always seemed puzzled when he didn't find anything on me, and he probably thought I'd very cleverly gotten rid of the loot somehow. I guess he just couldn't figure out why else a kid like me would hang around a big department store so much. I had my reasons, but I couldn't have explained them, even if I'd wanted to.

Of course, one reason was probably just that it was so handy. For a few years I shined shoes right outside the big glass and bronze doors of the east entrance, and from time to time I'd just stroll in—to get warm in bad weather, to see what was new, or just to catch up on the latest store gossip with a few friends I'd made among the clerks. Then when I began to outgrow the shoeshine business a couple of years ago, most of the new jobs I found were pretty much in the same area. Usually in the city a guy is pretty much out of luck from the time he outgrows the shoeshine and paperboy businesses, until he's sixteen and can be put on a payroll. But I'd made a lot of contacts while I was shining shoes, and I managed to do all right. Most of my jobs were pickup things that I'd developed into a regular schedule. I ran errands, washed display cases, cleaned up and did occasional stock room jobs—mostly in the smaller shops on Palm Street. Also, I still kept my shoeshine stuff at the flower stand, and even though I didn't shine shoes on the street anymore, I kept a few old well-paying customers who liked to have me come up to their offices to give them a shine. That whole area, around Eighth and Palm was kind of my territory and Alcott-Simpson's was right in the middle of it—in a lot of ways. I guess that's why, when all the trouble started at the store, I was right in the middle of that, too.

I think the trouble probably started early in January, and it was around the middle of the month that I first saw Sara. Before that time I *had* heard a rumor or two, but nothing definite; and I don't think the rumors were on my mind at all on that particular afternoon. If I had any special reason for walking through Alcott-Simpson's that day, it must have been partly that I wanted to see what the decorating theme was for the after Christmas sales. Alcott-Simpson's was practically famous for its display themes. But mostly I just wanted to get in out of the cold for a minute. Outside it was doing the Winter-Wonderland bit for real, and my jacket wasn't exactly mink, if you know what I mean.

The first thing I did was to drift over to a bench I knew about near the east entrance and sit down. The bench was in a little alcove behind Ladies Gloves where customers were supposed to get out of raincoats and boots and stuff in bad weather. Mrs. Bell, who worked in Ladies Gloves, knew me. She was a typical Alcott-Simpson clerk, a shell of perfect dignity hiding a heart of pure nothing, but she was friendly enough to warn me if Priestly or one of his boys were heading my way; so I used the bench behind Ladies Gloves quite a bit. Quite a few times I'd even curled up there and gone to sleep—when I'd been particularly tired and cold. But it was late that day and I only meant to stay there until I got warm and then go on home. I'd only been sitting there for about a minute though when I began to notice something.

I don't know exactly what it was I noticed. I don't remember seeing anything the least bit unusual. I didn't hear anything either, at least nothing definite—but maybe it did have something to do with hearing. It was as if the low hum of movement and conversation that you can always hear in a big place like that was on a different key, higher and faster, like the tuning was a little bit off. I was beginning to get the feeling that something was up, so instead of going on home I dropped in behind two fat ladies with a lot of packages and strolled down the aisle towards Cosmetics. I had a good friend in Cosmetics.

Madame Stregovitch lived near us in the Cathedral Street district, and she had worked at Alcott-Simpson's for years and years. I don't know why everybody called her Madame instead of Mrs., except that you just couldn't imagine calling her anything else. It went with her accent, and her personality, which was very positive. She'd been at Alcott-Simpson's so long that a lot of the important customers were convinced they couldn't get along without her, and for that reason she could do just about as she pleased. But she was the only one. Most of the clerks at Alcott-Simpson's wouldn't have sneezed without asking permission.

It's a funny thing, but when I first started hanging around, I used to think the Alcott clerks were something special. The way they dressed and acted, you got the feeling that they were all a bunch of eccentric aristocrats who were just working for the fun of it. You had to be around for a long time to find out what most of them were really like. Basically, most of them were a scared bunch of underpaid apple-polishers, who put up with all sorts of bullying just so they could go on associating with all that mink and money. At least, I guess that's the reason they did it. You'd have to have

9

some sort of hang-up to make you go on putting up with a lot of those A-S big shots and all the rules and regulations, the way the clerks at Alcott's did.

All except Madame Stregovitch. If there was any bullying going on around her, she was right in there doing her share of it. She even ordered her Rolls-Royce-type customers around, and nobody ever complained. They wouldn't dare. She affected everybody that way. It was just something about her that you couldn't exactly put your finger on.

When I got to Cosmetics that day, Madame was busy with a customer; but she saw me and arched an eyebrow in my direction. Madame's face was dark and sharp and full of bony edges. She almost never smiled, and her mouth hardly seemed to move even when she talked; but her eyes and eyebrows had a large vocabulary all by themselves. Right at the moment she was busy rubbing a drop of something on the cheek of a great big woman with a long nose, saggy eyes and a short brown fur—probably a beaver. (The coat I mean, anyone who hangs around Alcott-Simpson's can't help getting to know a lot about furs.)

"You see, my dear," Madame was saying in the soothing hum that she always used on customers, "how it brings out your delicate coloring." Madame doesn't have much of a foreign accent, but she clips off her words and arranges them a little differently than most people.

In a few minutes the big woman went away with a

dazed smile and a whole box of make-up stuff, and Madame came over to where I was waiting.

"Dion," she said, "I have missed you. You have not been to see me since Christmas. You have not been sick?"

"No," I said. "I've been around. I just haven't been coming in much. Not enough business the first of January. Nobody to hide behind when old Priestly makes his rounds."

"Mr. Priestly, pah!" Madame Stregovitch said, shrugging her shoulders and tilting her eyebrows to a disgusted angle. "He has greater things to worry about these days than one harmless boy. You must come and see me, as always. In the midst of so much falseness, one's eyes are gladdened by the sight of such glorious youth."

Actually, Madame Stregovitch wasn't as weird as she sounded sometimes. It's just that she got started raving about how good-looking I was, way back when I first used to visit her, when I was a skinny little crippled kid. Of course, I really knew, even then, that she was only trying to make me feel good, but I got a kick out of it anyway. Eventually it was just a routine we went through.

"Sure," I said, "me and Mr. America. As a matter of fact, I'm thinking of going into business. Like— EYES GLADDENED. TWO FOR THE PRICE OF ONE! It ought to beat shining shoes." I usually do all right wising-off around adults. It's only around kids my own

age that I get tongue-tied.

Madame Stregovitch just narrowed her eyes and nodded slowly. She always appreciated a joke that way. We talked for a few minutes more about various things and, when I started saying I'd better go, she got something out from under the counter and gave it to me.

When I first knew Madame, she used to work in Alcott's Sweet Shop, and we got in the habit of her always keeping something for me under the counter. In those days it was usually a piece of fudge or a gumdrop. But this time it looked like a few pages from a newspaper. "It is for your collection," she said. "I've been saving it for you since before Christmas."

I thanked her and started to unfold the paper, but just about then I caught a glimpse of a familiar face. It was one of the store detectives, a musclebound character named Rogers. He was always cruising around the store looking as neat and chummy as a penguin, but I'd discovered a long time before that he could lose his Alcott-Simpson manner in a hurry, when he was sure nobody important was looking. A couple of times when I was younger he'd escorted me out through one of the storerooms and sort of bounced me off a few walls along the way. I wasn't really afraid of him. I had learned not to allow myself to be taken out through a storeroom, without putting up a fuss— a fuss is something that all of Priestly's henchmen were trained to avoid at all costs. But Rogers was looking particularly determined, and I wasn't in the mood for an argument. So I nodded to Madame, tucked the paper into my pocket and started for the door.

But Rogers had a head start on me and he was coming as fast as humanly possible for someone who was supposed to pretend to be just another shopper. He was already past the escalator and shopping up a storm right through the middle of the Knit Shop. I saw right away that he was going to cut me off unless I broke into a run, and of course I wasn't about to do that. Alcott-Simpson's is the kind of place where no one would think of running unless his life depended on it; and personally, I probably wouldn't run if it did —because of my crummy limp. I'd just about resigned myself to an unpleasant discussion—at the very least— with old Rogers, when all of a sudden I realized he was after somebody else.

It was a girl. When I first saw her, she was looking back over her shoulder at Rogers and I couldn't see her face; but from what I could see, she was a typical Alcott customer. At least she was dressed like one. She was wearing high narrow boots, a kind of sleeveless thing of orangish suede and a cashmere sweater; all very latest fashion and expensive-looking. Her hair was long and straight and very black.

I'd hardly had time to wonder why on earth Rogers should be after her when she brushed past me in the aisle, so close I could have reached out and touched her—and I noticed something that really gave me a jolt. She was wearing the sweater just hanging over her shoulders, and on the empty sleeve there was a cardboard tag. It was an Alcott-Simpson price tag!

That could only mean one thing—and it was right then that I remembered the rumor I'd heard a few days before. José, at the flower stand, had told me that he'd heard from one of the Alcott janitors that there was a bunch of plainclothesmen hanging around the store, and that there was talk about some kind of gang of thieves and vandals.

As the girl turned the corner at the end of the next counter, she looked back at Rogers again, and I got my first real look at her face. It wasn't at all what I expected. I can't exactly explain why it was a shock, but it was. Actually, I don't know what kind of face I expected on a shoplifter, but I knew right away that this wasn't it.

She was quite young, for one thing. Maybe about my age, or even younger. And her skin was dark—not darker than a beach tan, maybe, but with a different shade to it, like a shadow of purple under the brown. But most of all I noticed her eyes. They were very big and dark—black, but clear and deep—like the night must be to a cat. For just a second she looked right at me and smiled like she thought the whole thing was a joke, and then she hurried on.

On the other side of Hosiery she turned quickly to the left, and I almost yelled at her to go the other way. If she had turned to the right, she just might have made it to the Palm Street entrance in time; but the way she was headed, she was walking right into a trap. Behind the hosiery counter there was only a short corridor that led to some storerooms, and the doors were always kept locked.

But I didn't yell, and the girl disappeared into the corridor and a few seconds later Rogers followed. I knew he had her then, and I could just imagine the smug look on his slick face. But the girl was obviously a thief all right, and that was her problem. There was no reason for me to get involved. I had plenty of troubles of my own. I told myself that the thing for me to do was to turn around and cut out, while Rogers was occupied. But I didn't, and when I reached the end of the hosiery counter, I met the great detective on his way back—all by himself. Behind him the short corridor was empty. The girl seemed to have completely disappeared.

It occurred to me that maybe one of the storeroom doors had been unlocked after all. But that didn't explain why Rogers came back so quickly, or the look on his face. I got a good look at him as he came back past me, without even glancing my way. His eyes were wide open but without any focus, like a sleepwalker looking at his dream.

Out on the sidewalk the wind was colder than ever and full of freezing mist. As soon as I picked up my stuff from José, I turned up the collar of my jacket and headed south towards Cathedral Street. I kept thinking about the girl on the way home.

Chapter 2

OUR HOUSE IS AN OLD VICTORIAN BROWNSHINGLE IN the Cathedral Street district. Matt Ralston, who studies sociology and lives in our attic, says the whole district is in what is called a "changing neighborhood," but I don't know what that means, because what neighborhood isn't? I mean, as long as there's people in it? But as far as our street is concerned, the change seems to be towards more kids on the sidewalks and less paint on the houses. And our house is no exception.

It must have been quite the thing when my dad's family built it, but it's pretty beat up now, and getting worse all the time. It has so many missing or crooked shingles that it looks like a moulting chicken, and the yard is bare except for clumps of mangy grass and broken toys and an iron pole with a sign that says James Music School—Second Floor. The toys belong to the Grovers who live on the first floor, and James is my father.

My dad is Arnold Valentine James, music teacher and neighborhood philosopher, known as Val to his many friends and students. He is also sometimes known as Prince Val. The "Prince" is as in "he's a Prince of a guy." He is also the world's worst business man and the most famous soft touch in this part of town. He really is a great music teacher, but he doesn't charge enough to make people think he's any good, and half the time he doesn't collect even what he does charge. He's always letting people give him some worthless piece of junk instead of money. As a matter of fact, when I was younger, I used to wonder some- times if that was how he got me. I couldn't remember my mother and I'd never heard much about her, so it occurred to me that maybe somebody with kids to spare got a little behind on his lesson payments and talked my dad into a trade. It wouldn't be the first time he got the worst of a deal.

Anyway, Dad and I live on only the second floor of the old house, now. The downstairs is rented to this family with three noisy little kids, and three uni- versity students live in the attic. The Grovers pay their rent most of the time, but the college guys only paid for four months last year; and so far this year they're still working on November—on the installment plan. Anybody but my dad would have kicked them all out a long time ago.

And besides not paying their rent, the whole bunch of them, at least the students and the kids, spend half their time in our apartment. The students come down to get away from the cold—there's not much heat in the attic; and the kids come up to get away from their mother who is the nervous type.

That day, the first day I saw Sara, was typical. When I got home, there were seven people, two cats and a dog cluttering up our apartment. My dad and Matt, the sociology student, were playing chess on the kitchen table. Phil and Duncan, the other two so-called collegians, were sitting in front of the fireplace playing a banjo and a guitar; two of the Grover kids were tearing around shooting each other with cap pistols; and in the studio somebody was trying to play a march on the piano. Tiger, the Grover's mutt, was leaning against the kitchen door and whining because somebody had just fed our cats, Prudence and Charity, and they wouldn't let him have any. Everybody was suspiciously glad to see me.

"Dion! Welcome home."

"Here's Dion."

"It's Dion."

"Hey look. It's the teen-age tycoon of Palm Street."

I looked around and just as I thought—even though it was almost six o'clock, there wasn't a sign of anything to eat around the place; unless you wanted to count the cat food. That probably meant it was up to me if there was going to be any dinner.

"Look Dad," I said, "I thought you were going

to collect from the Clements for sure, today."

"I tried, Dion. I went over there. But they've had a lot of illness——"

I slammed out of the room without waiting to hear the rest. It was a very old story. Every now and then towards the end of the month, I had to chip in with some of my money to buy stuff for dinner—or else go hungry. I didn't mind so much for Dad and me, but when it included everybody in the neighborhood who happened to be broke, it burned me up. Strictly speaking, it was usually just one or more of the guys from upstairs—but not always. My Dad would invite a perfect stranger with six inch fangs and three eyes up for dinner if he found him on the corner looking like he needed a square meal.

Out in the hall I let off a little steam by chasing the Grover kids and Tiger downstairs. The noise level went down several decibels right away. The kid in the studio kept forgetting to flat the same note. It was enough to drive you out of your skull, so I went in and chased him home, too. He wasn't there for a lesson anyway. My dad lets several neighborhood kids who don't have their own pianos at home come over to practice whenever they feel like it. Prudence and Charity weren't making any noise, but they'd finished their cat food so I threw them out, too—just for a finishing touch. By then I was feeling better so I went back into the kitchen.

"Look, Di," Matt said. (If you can picture Abra-

ham Lincoln with a curly blond beard, you've got
Matt to a T.) "We have some spaghetti and a fairly
youthful head of lettuce upstairs. If you could chip in
enough for some odds and ends for a meat sauce, et-
cetera, we'd be in business. And I'll finance a real feast
next week when my check comes."

"Sure you will," I said. "If you don't find some girl
to spend it on first."

"Not a chance. I've reformed." He grinned at me
coaxingly. "I'll shop, and we'll make Phil and Dunc do
the dirty work."

I weakened. I was tired and hungry, and Phil really
was a good cook. So I handed over a couple of dollars
and went in my room to rest and wait for dinner. I
kicked off my shoes and flopped down on the bed. My
room is way at the back of our floor. It's little and dark,
but I keep it sort of neat and peaceful looking, and no
one ever goes in there but me. I'd been saving money
for over a year to buy a Danish modern desk like one I
saw at Alcott-Simpson's, but I still needed about thirty
dollars. It was an executive type desk, big and solid
looking, and long enough to fill up all one end of my
room. I'd spent a lot of time lying there picturing how
great it would look, right at the end of my bed—big
and smooth and shiny; and I couldn't help thinking
that it might already be there if I didn't have to feed so
many scrounging renters.

But thinking of Alcott-Simpson's reminded me of
Rogers and the girl, and I went over that whole thing

again. But no matter how I looked at it, it just didn't make much sense. About the only explanation I could come up with was that the girl had unlocked the store-room door earlier, or else someone did it for her. But even that didn't explain why Rogers didn't go on into the storeroom after her. Finally, I'd gone over it so much that I was beginning to think in circles, so I decided to think about something else. That was when I remembered about the papers that Madame Strego-vitch had given me.

It was a few pages from the magazine section of the Sunday *Times*, with an article about Alcott-Simp-son's. A long time ago I'd started a scrapbook about the store, and of course I'd told Madame about it. Actually it had been quite a while since I'd added any-thing to the book, but since Madame had gone to the trouble to save it for me, I decided to tape it in. So I got the book out of my closet and opened it to the first empty page.

It was one of those five-and-dime store scrapbooks with the picture of a collie dog's head stamped on the front. Inside, there were no pictures on the first page —only some big careful printing that said: ALCOTT-SIMPSON'S THE GREATEST STORE ON EARTH—by Dion James. It was pretty stupid and childish, but I'd started it when I was only eight. After the fancy title page there were dozens of pages of pictures—some with corny comments written under them in green ink. They were mostly newspaper pictures, like a spread the *Times* did when Alcott's opened the remodeled mezzanine; plus some advertisements that I happened to think were particularly interesting. There was a magazine story that came out when the store had a big fiftieth anniversary and some nice slicks of display windows that Madame got for me from the art department. It was all put together very carefully and neatly and I could remember how much time I used to spend working on it or just looking over the pictures.

Actually, a lot of kids make scrapbooks—particularly a certain type of kid, like I was, who gets a kick out of saving and organizing stuff. The only difference is that most kids make books about airplanes or sports heroes or that kind of thing; I just happened to make one about a store. It's not as if Alcott-Simpson's was just any big city department store. I've been around quite a bit in the last few years and I've seen a lot more than I had when I was eight years old; and there just wasn't anything anywhere quite like it. It seems the original Alcott and Simpson were a couple of old millionaires who decided to build the world's most beautiful and luxurious commercial palace. The ground floor was divided into a lot of fancy little shops connected by a walk called The Mall. Then in the center there was a kind of indoor garden with a fountain and statues. The building covered an entire block and I used to think there wasn't anything in the world, worth having, that you couldn't buy there. After I'd been around for a while and looked at everything, I think that impressed me even more than the building itself —how many things you could buy there. Just about anything you could possibly want from diamond rings to motorcycles. Everybody who saw it for the first time was kind of overwhelmed, so you can imagine what it did for a kid who'd never had anything that cost more than five bucks—except for operations. As a matter of fact, I even used to dream about it.

It wasn't a dream, exactly. That is, I wasn't exactly asleep. It was that half-awake kind of dream—awake enough to start it on purpose, but near enough asleep not to know where it's going. It usually started out about how eight-year-old Dion James, shoeshine boy, had inherited the fabulous Alcott-Simpson department store from some kind old gentleman. Sometimes I thought it all out, how I'd done this old gentleman a favor, like pushing him out from in front of a bus, so he put it all down in his will about the whole store and everything in it going to me when he died. In my dream I never operated the store. I mean, I never sold anything. I just owned it and sort of lived in it. Sometimes, I brought in all my special friends and gave them stuff, like a new seven-foot Steinway grand for my father; but other times I was just there in the store all by myself, looking around and playing with the toys and stuff like that.

Of course, that was all in the past. I'd pretty much outgrown the daydreams along with scrapbooks. But I couldn't help being interested in the article that Madame Stregovitch had been saving for me. It really belonged in my scrapbook—it was so—kind of typical of Alcott-Simpson's. It was a feature article on some special luxury gifts that the store had been selling for the Christmas season.

The article started off humorously about how Alcott-Simpson's had opened a special department for people who wanted to buy a gift for the "Friend Who Has Everything" or even for the "Friend You Want to Flatter by Pretending to Think He Has Everything." There was a list of very expensive, very kookie gifts, and colored photographs of a few of the most spectacular. There were things like a diamond studded thimble, a solid gold toothbrush and a silver-mink bathmat. The last page had a big picture of the craziest of all, a mink-lined fishbowl.

That's what they called it, but of course, it wasn't meant for real fish. Some little golden fish and some imitation water plants were imbedded right in the glass walls of the bowl, and because the glass was thick and wavy, they were supposed to seem to be moving. You couldn't tell it from the outside at all; but if you looked in the top, you could see that the inside of the bowl really was lined with fur. The blurb under the picture called it a conversation piece and said that it cost seventy-five dollars.

I was starting to cut out the picture and thinking you'd have to be pretty desperate for something to talk about to buy a thing like that, when suddenly I saw this weird thing. Right in the center of the fishbowl there was a pair of eyes. The eyes were shadowy—but clear enough so I knew I couldn't be imagining them. I stared for a minute, and the eyes seemed to stare right back, vague and dim and sad-looking. And then suddenly I realized what I was seeing. The eyes were part of something on the other side of the paper.

I turned the page over and, sure enough, right on the back was a picture of a girl with great big eyes and stringy dark hair. When I had started to cut out the picture, I'd held it up so that the light from my lamp was right behind it and it made the eyes seem to come right through. I'd just had time to notice that it was a part of an article about some foreign country, when I heard Phil yelling at me that the spaghetti was ready.

I taped it into the scrapbook in a hurry—and that was that.

I don't think I thought much more about it then, but I do remember feeling more relieved than seemed to make sense under the circumstances. I mean, what other reason could there be for a pair of eyes in the midst of a mink-lined fish bowl?

Chapter 3

I STARTED OUT DINNER THAT NIGHT NOT SPEAKING TO my father. I was pretty burned up at him, not that there was anything particularly unusual about that. It seemed like I spent half the time not speaking to him, not that it ever did any good. As a matter of fact, I doubt if he even noticed most of the time. At least, if he did he was careful not to make an issue of it. That's one of his peculiarities. I doubt if he has ever made an issue out of anything in his life.

My dad is tall and blond, and if he weren't so unwarlike he'd look a lot like an old Viking warrior—and not a whole lot better groomed either. He's been kind of a neighborhood landmark in the Cathedral Street district for years and years. As a matter of fact, he was born right here in this house way back when this was a fashionable part of town; and he's always lived right here, except for some years he spent in Europe, studying music and drifting around, when he was young. His father was a professor at the university, and Dad still has some friends on the faculty. Actually, he has friends all over everywhere, but most of his students come from our neighborhood—and that's part of the problem. Nobody in our neighborhood has much money.

Just that morning before I left for school Dad and I had had a talk about finances; and he'd absolutely promised that he was going to collect some of the money that his students owed him. It was obvious what had happened. As usual, he'd listened to some sob stories and let himself be talked out of collecting. There was almost nothing he did that frustrated me more.

So, for a while I just stared at my plate and shoveled up the spaghetti, but before too long I had to thaw a little. For one thing the spaghetti sauce was really good, and for another our kitchen is a great place to eat dinner on a cold January night. It used to be the master bedroom once, when the house was a one family affair, so it has a big fireplace and a nice comfortable atmosphere. Besides, Phil and Duncan were clowning around as usual, and keeping a straight face got to be too much of an effort. Those two could make a corpse laugh.

Phil and Dunc came from the same little town somewhere out in the boondocks, and I guess they've been friends since they were practically babies. Their families don't have much money, so they're working their way through college by scholarships and odd jobs, and scrounging—like they do off my father. They're both nineteen years old and in their second year at the university; but they're not studying the same things. Dunc is taking art courses, and I'm not sure what Phil is doing. I asked him once, and he said he was studying to be rich. But as far as I can see, they both spend most of their time thinking up things to laugh at. That night they were doing something they called nationalistic spaghetti eating.

The way it worked, they took turns acting out how someone from a particular country would eat spaghetti and the rest of us were supposed to guess what nationality. First, Phil was a super-polite Englishman, whose monocle kept falling out and getting lost in the spaghetti. Then Dunc did a Chinese trying to eat spaghetti with chopsticks. Next Phil chopped up some spaghetti, mashed it all to pieces and finally put his plate on the floor and pretended to march back and forth across it. That was supposed to be a German. Another one was the efficient American trying to tie all the pieces of spaghetti together end to end so he could suck up the whole plate without stopping. It was all pretty corny, but the way Phil and Dunc throw themselves into a thing like that—you just can't help laughing. I had forgotten all about being mad, until Dad brought out the doughnuts.

When the spaghetti was all gone, my father got up and went over to this great big bread box we have and opened it up, and it was absolutely packed full of doughnuts. There must have been six or eight dozen—a lot more than we could possibly eat before they spoiled. All of a sudden I knew exactly where they came from.

Mr. Clements, who just happens to have two kids who take piano from Dad, and who just happens to owe us more money than anybody else, just happens to work at a big doughnut factory. And Joannie Clements just happened to tell me once that her father gets to take home any doughnuts that get a little old before anyone buys them.

Dad put about a dozen doughnuts on a plate and passed it around the table. I could tell that he was trying to keep from catching my eye, so at last I said, "How much did you knock off for this junk?"

Dad smiled in that vague way of his. "Just a little," he said. "But I did tell Dan that we might be able to use a few more from time to time."

That did it. I stood up and threw my half-eaten doughnut at Prudence, who was sitting in front of the fireplace washing her feet. I missed, but it was close enough to make her jump. She gave me a dirty look and then she sniffed at the doughnut, looked disgusted, and went back to washing her feet. Even the cat wouldn't eat them. "Good Lord, Dad," I said. "You don't even *like* doughnuts!" And I stormed out of the kitchen and back to my room.

That was the way it had been between my father and me for a year or two. Before that we got along pretty well. As a matter of fact, when I was a real little kid I used to think he was just about perfect. Of course, he was as easygoing with me as he is with everybody, and at that age you don't notice much else. He almost never got mad or ordered me around, but I wasn't so awfully spoiled, either. I think I sort of had the feeling that he expected me to act like some kind of small-sized adult and I just couldn't bear to let him down. He seems to have that effect on the little kids he teaches, too. It's only older people who take advantage of people like him.

Anyway, when I was little we used to have a lot of good times. I was only four when I had polio, and after that there were three operations a year or two apart, so I never did go to elementary school very regularly. I was home in bed or in a wheel chair a lot, and having the house always full of people seemed like a great thing to me, then. There were my Dad's students and his musician friends and his neighborhood friends and his chess friends and his political-enemy friends—not to mention the ones who showed up regularly just for a square meal or for someone to listen to their troubles. People were always drifting in for an hour or a day—or even a month or two if they happened to feel like it. Not many of them were kids, but in those days that didn't matter very much. There was always a lot of music going on, and I was right in the middle of it all the time. Dad had started me on the violin when I was almost a baby, and I took up the guitar, too, a few years later. When I was about six, I started thinking up lyrics and tunes to go with them, and Dad would write them down. All his friends were always carrying on about what a lot of talent I had.

That part of my life was okay in those days—school was the bad part. During the spells, in between operations, when I was well enough to go to Lincoln Elementary, I began to realize that I didn't exactly fit in. I couldn't play any sports, which was terribly important at Lincoln, and I didn't know how to make the right kind of conversation. And besides that I didn't dress right. A lot of the time Dad wouldn't even notice my clothes, and I'd go for days in outgrown, worn-out stuff. Then he'd decide to dress me all up in some out-of-date sissy suit that some old family friend had donated, and that was even worse. It got so I hated to go to school; and the more I hated it, the worse it got. But I never blamed anyone. Little kids are apt to be pretty fatalistic. You just take what comes, and it doesn't even occur to you to wonder if things are the way they ought to be or if you could do anything to make them better. It was in between my second and third operation that I started shining shoes and hanging around Alcott-Simpson's, and not too long after that I began to quit just accepting things and started making plans for the future—all sort of plans.

That night, after the doughnut episode, I shut myself in my room again and started in on my homework. I'd nearly finished my English assignment when there

was a knock on the door. I didn't even answer at first, but then I heard Matt's voice saying, "Di, it's Matt. Let me in."

Matt is a graduate student and he's older than Phil and Dunc—around twenty-three or four. He's been staying with us off and on for years. But being around for a few years doesn't really make him part of the family—even though he acts like he thinks he is at times. When I opened the door that night, he came on real casual-like, but I knew him too well to be fooled. I could tell he had something on his mind. He stretched out on my bed with his heels up on the footboard and started out like he'd just come to chat.

"How's it going?" he asked, nodding at my homework.

"Okay," I said. "It's just English. I got my algebra done in study hall." Sometimes Matt helped me out with my algebra when I hit a snag. I'm not too good at that sort of thing, and Dad's not much better.

Matt asked some more questions about the English assignment and we kicked that around for a while, but I had the feeling that he was looking for an opening for something in particular. Finally he looked around my room and said, "Very cozy. Sure is a nice pad, you've got here."

"Nothing special," I said. "It just looks good in contrast to the rest of the house."

Matt didn't say anything for a minute. Then he asked, "What's the matter with the rest of the house?"

"Oh, not a thing," I said. "If you like living in a disaster area."

Matt just raised one of his curly blond eyebrows at me and said, "Hmmm."

"Hmmm?" I asked. "Like, hmmm—as in what?" The way I said it was kind of sharp and sarcastic, because I was thinking to myself, "Here we go again with the 'big-brother' bit." Matt seems to think that just because he's known Dad and me for such a long time it gives him the right to tell me what to do. It always makes me angry, but at the same time I think I kind of like it—maybe because nobody else ever tries to tell me what to do very much and it sort of makes you feel somebody cares. Anyway, whenever Matt starts preaching I always get this, "Oh boy! Am I going to get mad this time " feeling.

Matt just grinned. "Hmmm as in—so that's it. So that's what's behind all this not-so-happily-ever-after-bit. You may not have noticed it, but lately you've been operating as if you were trying to set the whole togetherness program back by about one hundred years."

"I don't know what you're talking about," I said very coldly. And I didn't either, at least not entirely.

Matt stopped grinning. "All right," he said. "I'll draw you a picture. I happen to think you have a very nice old man, and I don't think much of the way you've been treating him."

"You're sure someone to talk," I said, and I was so

mad I couldn't keep my voice from wobbling. "At least I don't owe him three hundred dollars rent."

Matt nodded. "Right you are," he said, "you don't, and I do. However, there's nothing I can do about that right now except move out, and I don't think that would make matters any better for anybody. And, believe me Di, I *am* going to pay him back, and with interest. Money's a lot easier to pay back than some other things."

I walked over to the window and stood looking out at the brick wall two feet away across the air vent. "You can leave anytime," I said.

But he just sat there on the edge of my bed. He sat there and I stood there and looked out the window and waited, and finally he started talking again. "Look Di. I know how you feel."

That really burned me. I knew enough about Matt to know that he couldn't have a clue about how I felt. His father was a rich doctor and he'd been brought up with servants and everything. His folks were mad at him right at the moment because he wouldn't live like they wanted him to and study to be a doctor like his father. But he sure as hell *didn't* know what it was like to grow up in a sort of neighborhood soup kitchen and have to shine shoes so that you could have the kind of things most kids have handed to them on a silver platter.

"A lot of people want the kinds of things you're wanting." Matt went on. "As a matter of fact, a whole lot of people never discover there's anything else in life to want. So I'm sure not going to knock you for it. It's just that I don't think you're appreciating what a rare bird your father really is."

Suddenly I wasn't so mad anymore. I came over and sat down. "I know it," I said. "I know what he's like. But you can't count on him for anything. And it isn't as if he couldn't. He could get a steady job teaching at a high school or even a college if he wanted to. But he just likes it here. He likes it where he can go around looking as if he's slept in his suit all the time and nobody cares. I don't know what's wrong with him. Why isn't he more like—other people?"

Matt rubbed his beard. "I don't know, Di. I don't know why he's the way he is. I suppose it's probably some ignoble human reason, just like the ones that bug all the rest of us. It's just that his kind of reaction is in considerably shorter supply than most." He grinned at me. "Let's just say he's a natural born lame-duck hunter, and Cathedral Street just happens to be one of the best lame-duck covers in this part of the country."

Matt's crooked sorrowful grin can cool just about anybody. I didn't really mean to, but I smiled, too. "Yeah," I said. "That's for sure."

"And personally," Matt said, getting ready to go out the door, "personally, I feel pretty lucky to be one of your father's walking wounded."

I laughed. "I know what you mean. But you and Phil and Dunc aren't walking wounded."

38

"Sure I am. The lamest of the lame. I don't know about Phil and Dunc, though. They have their problems all right, but as far as I can see most of them are spelled Y O U T H."

"You're always talking like that—like you were about a hundred years older than Phil and Dunc."

"I am," Matt said. "I am. That's another myth this country believes in—that chronological age has anything to do with how old you are. Phil and Dunc aren't just young, they are young-young. I was older than that before I started kindergarten." Matt went out the door and stuck his head back in. "And so were you," he said.

I knocked off the rest of the English assignment and sat there for a while staring at nothing. I kept thinking about what Matt had said. It was true all right, particularly about the lame-ducks. People with serious problems just seemed to take one look at my father and say, "This is it!"

It hadn't occurred to me before, but I suddenly realized that that was what my mother must have been. I really didn't know too much about her or what her problems were, because Dad never seemed to want to talk about it; but from the little he had told me, I could imagine the whole story. She had been just another one of his lame-ducks, only she had married him; but when she found out he couldn't really help her very much, she walked out. And she left me behind, and I turned out to be the biggest lame-duck of all.

All of a sudden I was mad again, for some reason. All the time I was getting ready for bed I was fuming, throwing things around and slamming them down. In the bathroom, I kicked some dirty towels that were lying on the floor clear out into the hall. Then I clumped back to my room limping hard—I really don't *have* to limp at all anymore, except when I run. And after I was in bed I stared into the darkness, waiting angrily, as if sleep were somebody who had promised to be on time and then wasn't.

EVEN THOUGH I LAY AWAKE FUMING FOR A LONG
time, I got up very early the next morning. As a matter of fact I got up early nearly every week day so I
could spend an hour or so on my various jobs before I
went to school. I had certain places I was expected on
certain mornings, and I always showed up. I had to.
Most of my jobs were the kinds of things that the people who hired me could have done themselves or gotten along without, if they'd wanted to. So all I had to
do was miss a few times and they'd get out of the habit
of leaving it for me. Like, for instance, every Monday
and Thursday mornings I swept out the workroom at
Jayne Anne's Hat Shop and carried all the trash out to
the alley. The Hat Shop was too small to hire a janitor,
and Jayne Anne hated sweeping out—and I was always
handy, so she left it for me. But she really had plenty
of time to do it herself if she'd felt like it.

Anyway, it was three, four days later, the next
Monday after I first saw Sara, when I was on my way

Hat Shop, that I saw the police dogs. up Eighth Avenue on my way to the as I was passing the alley where the trucks into Alcott-Simpson's storerooms, I noticed a motion at one of the alley exits. I stopped and watched while two guys with big German Shepherds on leashes came out and got into a police car. When I got to the flower stand, I told José about it.

"Sure," he said. "Cop-dogs every night. Tree, four nights, now. Big store got big trouble." José grinned happily. The big shots at Alcott-Simpson's had tried to make him move his flower stand once, and he'd had it in for the whole store ever since. But I couldn't get much more out of him about what was going on, so that afternoon I paid another visit to Madame Strego-vitch to find out what she knew.

But even before I talked to Madame, as a matter of fact almost as soon as I got inside the big brass and glass doors of the east entrance, I began to get that feeling of something strange again. There was a difference in pitch, like before—but there was something else, too. Right at first I couldn't put my finger on exactly what it was.

Everything looked just the same as always. There was a pretty fair sized crowd of shoppers for a Monday afternoon, the floors gleamed, the fountain sparkled, and the air was full of that special Alcott-Simpson perfume—Essence of New-and-Expensive. The clerks stood around like always, looking neat and dressy and superior, except— It was just about then that I noticed that there was something different about them—they were noticing me. Except for a few friends, and now and then someone who'd been told to keep an eye on me, most of the clerks never seemed to notice that I was around at all. I didn't take it personally. Nearly everyone who just walked in cold got the old invisible treatment, unless they were dripping with mink or some other kind of wearable bank statement. It wasn't anything to get touchy about. The clerks just didn't want to get tied up with some sightseer and maybe miss a live one. Actually, you couldn't blame them.

But that day things were different. As I walked down the Mall towards Cosmetics, every clerk I passed who wasn't busy with a customer gave me her full attention until I got by. And not just me, either. That day the clerks were noticing everybody—and the way they were doing it sort of gave you the feeling that someone had just told them that Jack the Ripper was coming in disguise.

When Madame Stregovitch saw me, her eyebrows flared up and she went off into one of her fancy greetings. "Ahhh! The shadows are lifting. It is the Golden One, the Adonis of Eighth Avenue."

"Hey, I like it," I said. I got out my little notebook that I kept track of my job money in and pretended to write it down. "Let's see. How did that go? Adonis, A—D——" But as soon as we got through kidding around, I got right down to what I'd come to ask. "By the way, how about letting me in on the big mystery. I mean, what's going on around here anyway?"

Madame had been looking down at a tray of lipsticks she was arranging, but when I said that her eyes whipped around to me so hard and fast that for a minute I started to stammer. It happened to me all the time with kids, particularly girls, but hardly ever with adults—especially Madame. But when she wanted to, she had a look that could really nail you—like a bug on a pin.

"I—I mean, the police and dogs and everything. José's been saying the store has some kind of big trouble. I just wondered if you'd heard anything."

After a minute Madame nodded and went back to fixing the lipsticks. "Yes," she said." I have heard a little. There have been extra detectives hired and more guards at night. There is always some trouble in a big store like this. Perhaps it is the guards themselves. They say most of the damage has been done at night."

"You mean stuff has been stolen more than once at night, and no one can find out how anyone's getting in? Sounds like it *must* be the guards, or someone who's working with them. What are they taking? And how come it hasn't all been in the paper?"

Madame shrugged. When Madame shrugged, everything got in on the act—her eyebrows, her chin, her hands and even her nose; and her shrugs said a lot more than other people's. This one said that the store officials were idiots, that the whole thing was a big

44

joke, that there was nothing to worry about—but then right at the end her eyes came back to me and sharpened, and the shrug ended up saying something like, "Too many questions can get you in trouble." It felt almost like a threat. But out loud all she said was, "I think, actually, very little has been stolen." She reached under the counter and brought out some fudge. "See, your favorite from the Sweet Shop. Just like old times."

It was obvious that for some reason Madame didn't want to talk about it any more, but I was still curious; so when she went back to her customers, I decided to cruise around a bit just to get the feel of things. I happened to be wearing some of my best stuff, so I didn't figure I'd attract any special attention, unless I ran into Rogers or Priestly or one or two of the others who knew me.

I toured the main floor first. I walked all the way around the Mall, which was just a wide aisle lined with potted plants. On the inside was the indoor garden and fountain and some lounging areas where shoppers could sit down to rest their feet. And all around the outside were the different departments—some of them fixed up like separate little shops. There were dozens of them—Gifts and Notions and Cosmetics and Books and Jewelry and Silver and Stationery and Hobbies and Hosiery and the Travel Shop and the Gourmet Shop and the Import Shop and the Music Shop and the Art Shop and the Sweet Shop and the Flower

45

Shop, and a lot of others. Then all along the south side there was the Alcott Tea Room, which was indoors like everything else, but was designed to look like some kind of lawn party, with umbrella tables and potted trees.

I went all the way around the floor without seeing anything out of the ordinary, except for the way the clerks were acting. There did seem to be a few more men shoppers than usual; they may or may not have been extra store detectives.

Next I got on the elevator and went to the second floor. I didn't get off at the mezzanine because it was absolutely impossible not to be conspicuous there. It was where they had the best ladies' clothing and there was nothing on the whole floor but some chairs and couches sitting around on a practically knee-deep rug, plus a few artistic objects like pictures and statues. The idea was, you were supposed to tell the clerks—a bunch of dowager types in black dresses—what you had in mind and they trotted out some models wearing things you might like. I never could see just how it worked because the models were all nearly skin and bones and most of the customers weren't, but that wasn't my problem.

The second floor was clothing, too, only not quite so exclusive, and the third floor was one of my favorites —boys' and mens' clothing and the sporting goods department. I strolled around for a while on each floor, but I didn't see anything else that looked fishy. So I went up to the toy department on the fourth floor.

At one time I used to think that Alcott's toy department was just one step below Paradise—but that was when I was a kid. I hadn't even been there for several weeks, but right away I got the feeling that something was different. It hit me as soon as I stepped off the escalator. For one thing, there didn't seem to be nearly as many clerks as usual, and for another there was a new detective staked out between dolls and stuffed animals. He was all dressed up in an expensive tweed suit and he was kind of half-heartedly pretending to be shopping, but it was pretty much wasted effort. There are some cops who have COP written all over them so loud and clear that you couldn't mistake them if they were wearing lace negligees.

But, at least, since the guy was new he wouldn't recognize me, so I just got into the act and pretended to shop, too. First I looked into a junior planetarium that cost around two hundred dollars, and then I checked out a practically life-sized plush tiger that was a bargain for eighty-five. I was still putting on an act for the benefit of the tweedy cop—like I was some rich kid trying to decide what to buy for my little brother's birthday—when I saw Mrs. Jensen coming out of the toy department office. The office was in the storage area behind the children's book department, and the door was camouflaged with a book shelf to keep customers from strolling in by mistake. Mrs. Jensen is quite an old lady and she'd been the head buyer for the toy department for years and years—so of course, I knew her pretty well. She wasn't the kind of person you could kid around with, but she'd been patient with me all those years when I used to visit Alcott's toy department almost every day. I hadn't seen her for quite a while, though, so I decided to step over and say hello, and maybe get her version of what was going on.

When I came around the corner of the display case where I'd seen Mrs. Jensen go, she was squatting down counting something in the storage bins under the case. I came up behind her, but she didn't seem to hear me and I didn't want to interrupt her counting so I just picked up a model car that was on top of the case to look at while I waited for her to finish. It was one of those beautifully-made intricate miniature models, all real steel and chrome with real rubber tires. I was crazy about them when I was a kid, but I got pretty well bored with the thing that day while I waited. Mrs. Jensen finally seemed to have finished her counting, and she was just staring straight ahead as if she was thinking or trying to figure something out. At last I got impatient and gave a little cough to get her attention.

I *was* standing pretty close to her, but it wasn't a loud cough and I certainly didn't expect a reaction like the one I got. Like I said, Mrs. Jensen is an old lady, but she shot to her feet like a five-year-old and whirled around with her hand up to her throat. A funny little scream, more like a strangled squeak, came out of her mouth and her eyes behind the rimless glasses looked faded with fright.

She saw me then, and in the next few seconds her expression went from blind terror—to recognition—to relief—to embarrassment—to anger. It would have been funny except that she'd scared me almost as much as I'd scared her. I mean, it's kind of nerve-racking to be screamed at for nothing at all, and besides it occurred to me that maybe she was going to clutch her heart and topple over—and it would all be my fault.

But she didn't have a heart attack, after all. Instead she started bawling me out. "Dion," she said when she finally got her voice back, "what do you mean sneaking up behind people! What do you mean—" She noticed the model car in my hands then and she reached out and snatched it away. "What do you mean handling things? Wearing things out? No wonder things are getting broken. No wonder things are scuffed and shopworn before they've been on the shelves a day. No wonder—"

She was still sputtering along like that when a deep voice interrupted, "Is something the matter, Mrs. Jensen?" And there stood the tweedy cop who had stopped pretending to be a customer and was standing over me, kind of twitching the way a cat does just before he pounces.

Seeing the cop standing there seemed to bring Mrs. Jensen back to her senses a little. "Why—why—no," she stuttered. "It's only that Dion here came up

49

behind me and startled me. I know the boy. It's all right." She managed a very wobbly smile. "It's perfectly all right, Mr. Crane." She took me by the elbow and started steering me out of the department. "I'm sorry, Dion," she said on the way out. "I don't know what came over me to make me act that way. It's just that I'm tired—and nervous. Things haven't been—that is, things haven't been going well in the department lately. I'm just not myself. I'm sorry I scolded you so." We'd gotten to the beautiful handcarved archway of elves and animals that led into the toy department. Mrs. Jensen turned loose of my elbow, and I started off.

"Well, good-by, Mrs. Jensen," I said.

"Good-by, Dion," she said. "Oh, by the way. I almost forgot in all the—" she smiled kind of sheepishly, "—excitement. Did you want something? Could I help you with something?"

"No," I said. "Not really. I was just going to say hello. I haven't been around for quite a while, so I thought I'd just say—hello."

"Oh," Mrs. Jensen said, and her smile was finally back to normal. "How nice of you, Dion. Hello to you, too."

"Yeah," I said, "Hello." And I left.

I went on up through Housewares without noticing anything else strange, but I kept thinking about Mrs. Jenson and wondering what had gotten into her to make her act so jumpy. She'd always seemed like a pretty calm person before.

I was about to get on the escalator to go up to the sixth floor, Furniture and Antiques, when I heard the closing bell ring. That meant it was five-thirty and time I stopped playing Sherlock Holmes and went home to dinner. But just a few minutes later, right at the very moment that I stepped on the down escalator on the second floor, suddenly all hell broke loose somewhere below me on the mezzanine.

The escalator was crowded with a closing time rush of downward bound customers, and the first scream seemed to freeze everyone still. But at the second scream, everyone suddenly decided that the escalator was moving too slow and started to run up or down. Probably the curious ones were trying to get to where the scream came from to see what had happened, and the scarier ones were trying to go in the opposite direction. But since it was hard to tell where the sound had come from, both types seemed to be heading both ways. Whatever they had in mind, what they actually accomplished was a kind of mass wrestling match, on a moving escalator. But the escalator kept going down, so eventually we all got dumped on the mezzanine landing.

The mezzanine was full of people running in all directions. As soon as I got untangled from the crowd, I got behind a statue of a Grecian lady and surveyed the scene. Fur-coated customers, black-dressed sales ladies and plain-clothed detectives were whizzing by like

crazy. But it was so noisy I couldn't hear what anyone was saying, and I couldn't make any sense at all out of what was going on. There were a couple more screams, not quite so loud, in the direction of the dressing rooms and then a janitor came running by carrying something that looked like a big butterfly net.

The whole thing was so interesting that it never occurred to me I might get myself in trouble by hanging around, until I saw Mr. Priestly getting off the elevator. I'd only gotten behind the Venus, or whatever it was, to keep out of the flight pattern; but all of a sudden I realized how it would look. There I was, a guy who was already suspected of being a troublemaker, if not a shoplifter, hiding behind a statue on a floor where goodness knows what had just happened. And to make matters worse, I suddenly remembered the tweedy cop in the toy department. He'd probably be only too glad to testify that I'd just been scaring the buyer in the toy department half to death—even if she was too nice to press charges. It didn't sound good. In fact, it even sounded suspicious to me, and I *knew* I was innocent.

Priestly was pretty close to me when I saw him, but he was looking the other way, towards the dressing rooms. I wasn't positive, but I didn't think he'd seen me—not yet, anyway. I eased out from behind the statue and started to stroll back towards the escalator. I couldn't get to the down one without going right past him, so I took the up one, thinking that I'd go up a few floors and then catch the elevator straight down to the street floor.

I don't know why I went clear up to the sixth floor before I crossed over to the elevators, except I was thinking that if I got on up there I'd be clear at the back of the elevator and all the people who got on at the floors in between would hide me from view when we stopped at the mezzanine.

No one else in the whole store seemed to be going up, so I kept on going up all by myself: third, fourth, fifth. And when I got off at the sixth floor, everything seemed to be deserted there, too.

As I walked across to the elevators, I didn't see a single person on the whole floor. Either the salesmen had gone home already, or else they had been called down to help with the emergency on the mezzanine. I pushed the *down* button and waited.

I was thinking hard about something—the scream, I guess. I was trying to figure out what had caused it. It didn't seem like something being stolen could cause that sort of scream, not even if it had been the Hope Diamond. It hadn't been an angry scream, or even outraged, that scream had been *fear*. I'd gotten about that far in figuring it out, when I realized that I'd been waiting quite a while. I checked the little pointer above the door and all of a sudden it dawned on me that the elevators had quit running.

My watch said six o'clock. I'd known that it was a little past closing time, but I hadn't thought it was that much. That meant I'd have to risk the escalator, and I was on my way back to it when I heard men's voices—it sounded like two or three of them on their way up. I whirled around and hurried in the opposite direction. It had occurred to me that there was one more way downstairs. So I dashed off across the huge floor, ducking around highboys and love seats, thinking to myself that it was a good thing I knew about the emergency staircase.

The emergency staircase was clear across the building from the escalators, and on the sixth floor it was in a little hall right between two of the furniture display rooms. There were a lot of display rooms fixed up to look like different rooms in houses—living rooms, dining rooms and so forth—but I knew just which two to look for. I ducked in between a red and white bedroom and an orange and yellow dining room, and there it was—the door to the stairway. The only thing was—it was locked.

I'd been scared before, but there was something about jerking on that locked door that made me push the panic button. I could hear the voices coming closer across the floor, and the word TRAPPED kept flashing across my mind like one of those blinking billboards. I had a crazy urge to do something, anything, in a hurry —and what I did was pretty stupid. I ducked into the red and white bedroom and slid under the bed.

Chapter 5

I'VE HEARD THAT YOUR WHOLE LIFE CAN PASS BEFORE your eyes in a few minutes when you're about to die, and I can believe it. I know for a fact that an amazing amount of insignificant stuff can shoot through your mind when you're only trapped under a bed on the sixth floor of a closed department store. As I lay there and listened to the voices of the men coming closer and closer, all sorts of useless thoughts popped into my mind. I don't remember most of it, but I do remember realizing that if I had to spend the night there, under that bed, my dad wouldn't even miss me until way after midnight. This little chamber orchestra that he plays with had a date to play for some women's club way out in the suburbs, and he wouldn't be home until late. Of course, the guys from upstairs would probably be down, particularly if it turned out to be a cold night. They came down to study by our fireplace whenever they felt like it, even when we weren't there; but they wouldn't worry about me. For all they knew,

I might be at the movies or spending the night with a friend.

I don't know why, but realizing that no one would be worrying about me made me feel worse than ever. It didn't make sense. If my dad was home and worried, all he could do would be to call the police. And the kind of mess I was in wasn't the kind of thing you wanted to be rescued from by the cops.

I could hear the two men doing something not far away. They were moving around from place to place as if they were checking to see if everything was ready for the night. Now and then I caught bits and pieces of their conversation—enough to know they were just salesmen, not detectives with dogs—and enough to tell that they were discussing what had happened on the mezzanine.

Once I heard one of them say something about "—nothing to get excited about. Whether she admits it or not, that girl in the Pet Shop must have let it get out." The other voice came from farther away and it sounded fast and jittery, as if he were pretty excited. I couldn't hear much of what he was saying, but when he finally stopped the closer voice answered, "That's a lot of nonsense. The old gal must have been hysterical or off her rocker. It must have been in there all the time and she just didn't notice it. It couldn't have been flying."

The jittery voice had moved closer. "Well," it said, "she seemed so positive. But I suppose it might have climbed up the wall and she saw it falling off and imagined it was flying."

"Sure," the first voice said, "there's bound to be a logical explanation."

They both moved away then, and after a while it got very quiet and most of the lights went off. As I began to calm down a little, I began to notice that I was very uncomfortable. The bed was so low that I had to stay flat on my face. I couldn't raise my head more than an inch, and some kind of a metal cross bar was pressing into my back. The air was stuffy; the dust in the thick rug choked me so that every few minutes I had to fight back a sneeze.

But in spite of the discomfort, I knew that getting up my nerve to crawl out into the huge open emptiness of the store was not going to be easy. And crawling out would be only the beginning. After that would come getting down six flights. The escalator would be stopped, but I might be able to walk down it. Then, there would be goodness knows how many watchmen and cleaning crews and policemen with dogs—not to mention getting out of the building through doors that would probably be locked from the inside as well as from the out. With all that to worry about, it wasn't any wonder that it seemed easier just to lie there, at least for the moment.

I told myself that I had to start planning—deciding what I was going to do—but for a long time all I seemed to be able to do was torture myself with "if only" possibilities. "If only" I hadn't waited so long for the elevator before I realized it had stopped running; "if only" I'd risked being seen by Mr. Priestly and taken the down escalator in the first place; "if only" I'd tried to bluff it out with the two salesmen instead of hiding, like telling them I'd been in the men's room and hadn't realized the store was closing.

But the chance to do any of those things was gone, and when I came right down to it there were only two things left that I might do. One was to stay there under the bed all night and hope to go out in the morning with the early shoppers. And the other was to crawl out now and start trying to find a way out without being seen. The only problem was that knowing about the extra watchmen and the dogs made me pretty sure I wouldn't be able to make it either way.

There was one other possibility that came to mind, but I didn't consider it even for a minute. That was to go looking for the nearest guard and turn myself in, explain as well as I could, and face the music. Of course, there wasn't a chance that they would believe all of my story, but they might believe part of it, and because I was a first offender they might let me off pretty easy. However, I'd never be able to set foot inside Alcott-Simpson's again. Like I say, I didn't consider it for a minute. Somehow I was going to have to find a way to get out without being caught.

I don't know how long I lay there trying to get up my nerve to make a move, but it seemed like half a lifetime. I thought about the dogs a lot—what it would be like to be found by one—a huge shaggy head with long gleaming fangs lunging in towards me from the side of the bed. I pictured it coming in from different spots around me and each time the part of me closest seemed to shrivel in expectation. But for a long time I didn't hear anything that sounded at all like a dog, and after a while I began to worry about other things.

As time went by it got quieter and quieter, and as it did I began to listen harder and harder. The faint sounds of the city seemed a thousand miles away, and I could almost feel all the dark floors of the store stretching out around me like a huge deserted city. Then I began to think again about the screams on the mezzanine and what I'd overheard the salesmen say. I thought about what it could have been that could "crawl up a wall" and frighten someone enough to cause a scream like that. I even began to imagine things crawling in towards me under the edge of the bedspread—horrible vague things that crawled up walls and maybe flew——

Then I began to hear things. First I heard footsteps. Not like a watchman's feet, firm and heavy, but a light quick brush of sound that seemed very near and yet so soft that I couldn't be absolutely positive. Then there were voices that were the same way—whispers so soft that I never quite got to the point where I said, "There, that time I know I heard it." But once, without hearing anything, something made me turn my head and I saw the fringe on the bedspread swaying as if it had just been touched.

After that I lay there absolutely frozen for several minutes, but nothing more happened and the soft sounds seemed to have gone away. I was just beginning to tell myself that it had all been caused by the strain of waiting and that I had to pull myself together and crawl out, when suddenly very close to me a soft but very distinct voice said, "Hello."

I jumped so hard that my head bounced off a metal mattress support and my face ricocheted off the floor. For a minute I was blinded by the pain in my nose and the dust in my eyes, but I could hear all right and what I heard was the same soft voice saying, "Oh, did you hurt yourself? Are you all right?"

When I managed to get my sight back, I saw what looked like a girl's face, upside down in a pool of dark hair. As a rule I don't even have the nerve to be nice to girls, but I guess a hard bump on the nose can really affect your personality, at least temporarily.

"Oh sure," I growled. "Except for a concussion and a broken nose. What do you think you're doing anyway?"

The face disappeared for a minute. In the meantime the pain began to fade, and I began to get back to normal. When the face came back, I kind of quavered, "What do you want?"

That's the kind of stupid remark that's my usual speed around people my own age, but at least this girl didn't make things any worse by laughing or making a crack. She didn't try to answer my stupid question, either. What she said was, "I'm Sara." Actually, she didn't say Sara, exactly. At least not the way it's usually pronounced. The "r" was softer and sort of swallowed. But Sara is as close as I can get to it.

After a minute I said, "Hi" or "Hello" or some such remark.

"Who are you?" she asked.

"I'm Dion. Uh—Dion James. What are you doing here? Did you get shut in, too?"

She just went on looking at me for a while without answering, and then she said, "You'd better come out from under there. They always look under the beds."

"Yeah," I said, "I was afraid they would. But I didn't have much time to pick a place." I remember that right about then I was getting a surprised and hopeful feeling that maybe she wasn't going to turn me over to the guards—that maybe she even meant to help me.

62

"Can you get out?" she asked.

I began to try to scoot out, but the bed was awfully low. It's really amazing what you can do if you're scared enough. I couldn't remember having any trouble getting under the bed at all. I wiggled and puffed for a minute without making much progress until the girl reached under and got hold of my foot. She pulled and I pushed and before too long I was out.

It wasn't until then, when I saw her face right side up, that I realized who she was and where I'd seen her before. The light was dim where we were, but it was bright enough for me to be pretty sure it was the same girl I'd seen Rogers chasing a few days before on the main floor. She was dressed differently, but I was sure I remembered the eyes and the smile and the long black hair. Instead of the suede jumper, she had on a short shiny skirt with a low belt and a matching blouse with long tight sleeves. She looked very expensive and stylish, except that around her shoulders there was something white and pink and frilly that didn't seem to go with the rest of it. The frilly thing had slid around while she was helping me, and when she noticed that I was looking at it she started straightening it out. She had very small hands—very brown—and there was something about the careful way she touched the lacy stuff that made it obvious she really liked the way it looked. When she got it straightened out, I could see it was one of those little jackets that women wear in the hospital or when they're having breakfast in bed—I'd seen them in the movies and places like that. This one was one big mass of ribbons and lace and little pink flowers.

She said, "Isn't it beautiful?" The way she said it wasn't the way most girls would talk about something they were wearing. It was more the way you'd talk about a sunset or something.

"Yeah, nice," I said. "But look. Hadn't we better be getting out of here before we get caught?" But then all of a sudden it occurred to me that maybe she belonged there in some way. She looked too young to be an employee, but maybe she was the daughter of one of the big shots who was working late or something like that. She certainly didn't seem as worried as you'd think a young girl trapped in a closed department store would be. As a matter of fact, she didn't seem anywhere near as worried as I was.

She finished fixing the jacket and smoothed her hair down before she answered. Her hair was very thick and almost to her waist, and when she moved her head it slid around on her shoulders—soft and heavy like black silk. Her face was smooth and even, the kind that looks best with straight plain hair. In the half-light it seemed to have a kind of patterned perfection that was almost weird, like a planned design or a face seen through crystal. After a minute she said, "We'll have to find you a place to hide."

She looked all around and then she nodded and said, "Stay there a minute." She ran out of the display room and disappeared around the corner. She was back before I even had a chance to start worrying; and she was carrying a comforter, one of those fluffy satin quilts stuffed with feathers. She turned back the top of the bedspread and took out the pillows and told me to lie down across the bed where the pillows had been. It was a king-size bed so I just about reached across it from side to side without hanging over. She folded the quilt into a long fat roll and tucked it over me and patted it into the same shape the pillows had made. Then she pulled the spread back where it had been. "It looks just the same," she said. "Lie still."

"Hey," I said, but I heard her running again, out of the room.

For a minute or two I lay there in an absolute panic. It had all happened so fast and the girl had seemed so sure of what she was doing that I just went along with her, but suddenly I began to see the loopholes. It was a good hiding place, all right, if it weren't for the dogs, but they wouldn't be fooled for a minute. And what was going to happen to the girl? I was about to jump up and make a run for it when all at once she was back.

"Shhh," I heard her whisper. "I'm back. I had to put the pillows with the others so they wouldn't be noticed. Are you all right? Can you breathe?"

"Pretty well," I said. "But what about the dogs? And what are you going to do?"

"I have another hiding place. I'll go there in a

minute. Don't worry about the dogs. They won't find you. There are ways of making them go other places. They'll come soon with the men, and then they'll go back downstairs. When it's safe, I'll come back and show you how to get out of the store. Just remember not to move until I come back."

She was quiet then and I wasn't sure whether she was still there. I whispered, "Sara."

She said, "yes," from very nearby. I decided she must be sitting on the floor near the head of the bed.

"You'd better go. They'll find you there."

"I'll go soon, when it's time. The others will tell me."

I was thinking about that, wondering if she'd said what I thought she said and what it meant, when suddenly I felt her touch the spread over my head. "I'm going now. Don't move."

I lay there, trying to listen through the thick quilt and stuff over me. It seemed like years but it probably was only a few minutes before I heard voices. There were two or maybe three men, and they were going back and forth across the floor. They came closer and I heard another noise—a sharp whining bark. It was quiet for a while, and then there was more whining and voices giving commands. The dogs went on whining and whining, but they didn't seem to be getting any closer—and then I heard someone walk right into the room where I was hidden.

I held my breath and hoped that the quilt would

muffle the sound of my heart pounding. I could hear a man moving around, but no dogs' sounds, up close at least. In fact, the dogs were still whining now and then someplace quite a ways off on the other side of the floor. Finally the bed moved a little as if the man had put his hand on it as he got down to look underneath. "No sign of anything here!" he called a minute later, and then I heard him go on to the next display room.

Things had been quiet again for quite a while when I heard Sara's voice saying, "All right, you can come out now."

After we'd fixed the pillows back the way they'd been before, I said, "Okay, how do we get out?"

"Do you want to go right now?" Sara asked.

I guess I stared at her. The way she said it, it was like she thought I might want to sit down and play a hand of cards first or something.

"Well, I'm not exactly looking forward to the trip downstairs," I said. "But waiting around isn't going to make it any better. No telling when they'll be back with the dogs."

Sara thought a minute. "They'll go to the employees' room now and drink coffee. In an hour they'll take the dogs around again. But you're right. Now is the best time. Come on, we'll go this way."

She started towards the emergency staircase, so I told her that it was locked. She only said, "I think it will be open now." And it was.

At the top of the stairs we stopped and stood for a while listening. All of a sudden she said, "Now— hurry."

We ran all the way, and when we got to the ground floor we stopped and listened again, and then she led the way through a storage room that I recognized as one Rogers had dragged me through once. At the door that led out into the alley, she stopped.

"Aren't you coming, too?" I asked.

She shook her head. "I can't," she said, "because of the others."

Chapter 6

IT WASN'T EXACTLY THE KIND OF THING THAT HAP-
pens to just everybody, and for several days I thought
about it a lot. I went over it and over it in my mind—
the scream, getting locked in, the dogs and why they
hadn't found me, and the girl.

Sara was a real puzzle. Who she was and how she
happened to be in the store after closing were the biggest questions; but I also wondered about why she
bothered to help me, and how old she was, and if I'd
ever see her again. The way I remembered her, she
was really beautiful—dark and foreign looking, with
perfect skin and teeth and eyes like something from
outer space. She had that way of moving some girls
have, soft and bendy, like their bones have some rubber in them. But, she *did* look awfully young at times,
as if she might be only twelve or so—more of a little
kid than a girl.

The next few days I dropped by the store every
afternoon and took a quick look around; but I didn't

see anything new. And I didn't see Sara, either. And meanwhile, something turned up at home that gave me something else to think about for a while.

The thing that happened at home had to do with a letter, a letter about a job that my dad could have had if he'd wanted it. Well, actually it wasn't entirely a sure thing. Nobody gets handed a job they haven't even applied for. That was what really burned me up, Dad didn't even intend to apply. In fact, I wouldn't even have found out about it if I hadn't just happened to run across the letter. But I did find the letter and I read it and I made a scene about it; not that it did any good. Afterwards I wished I'd never even seen the letter, and I wouldn't have if it hadn't been for Mrs. Grover's nervous headaches.

When the Grovers moved into our downstairs flat, they made an arrangement with Dad for Mrs. Grover to clean our apartment once a week, and in exchange they got a big hunk taken off the rent. Well, the Grovers still pay the low rent, but recently Mrs. Grover's headaches have gotten worse, especially on Tuesdays when she's supposed to be cleaning our apartment. Oh, she usually makes it up, all right, but she's discovered what a good listener my dad is. I'm not there on Tuesdays, but the guys upstairs are in and out and they say that any minute Dad isn't busy with a student, Mrs. Grover corners him and starts crying into her dust cloth about her headaches and life in general. Anyway, the result is the house isn't much cleaner at the end of the day, so once in a while I try to straighten things up.

That's what I was doing that Sunday morning when I ran across the letter from the Wentworth School. It was lying there wide open, on top of the usual pile of debris that covers my dad's desk: unpaid bills, unsharpened pencils and unfinished symphonies. So I read it, and at first I was all excited.

Wentworth is a private high school out in the suburbs on the north side, and John Hubell, who is one of Dad's oldest friends, has taught music there for years and years. There was going to be an opening in the music department, so John had recommended Dad. And the headmaster was willing to consider him. The salary wasn't terrific, but it would be steady and a lot better than promises and stale doughnuts; best of all, we'd have to move. At least that's the way I looked at it. I charged into the kitchen where Dad was making a pot of lentil soup, waving the letter over my head.

"Hey," I babbled, "why didn't you tell me? Did you get it? When do you start?"

Dad looked at the letter and then he looked at me and then he went over to the table and sat down and started lighting his pipe. Lighting his pipe slowly and thoughtfully while you wait for an answer is one of the most maddening things he does. Finally he got it lit and took a deep puff and let it out slowly before he said, "You'd like for me to teach at Wentworth?"

It occurred to me just about then that John was

always complaining about what a lousy place it was to teach. It's a private school for girls, and according to John the girls are mostly spoiled brats and the administrators are a bunch of two-bit tyrants.

"Well, it's a steady salary," I said. "And if it's as bad as John makes out, why doesn't he quit?"

"John has a family, and he doesn't have his degree," Dad said. "It would be hard for him to find a job anywhere else. Besides, the time for John to break away has passed. He's been at Wentworth too many years. . . ." Dad took the pipe out of his mouth and put it down on the table, where he'd probably forget it and let it go out. "I have a great deal of sympathy for John's situation, but not enough to make me want to share it, I'm afraid. And the salary is really not a consideration. By the time I paid for transportation, it would be very little more than I'm making now. But I certainly didn't realize that you'd be so enthusiastic. It didn't occur to me—"

There were a lot of things that didn't occur to Dad where I was concerned. I shrugged and mumbled something about thinking maybe we could move to the north side. But I didn't wait for an answer. It was pretty plain that Dad had already turned down the chance to teach at Wentworth, so that was that. He was starting in on some of his reasons for not wanting to sell the house as I left the kitchen. I'd heard them all before.

Out in the hall I stumbled over Charity, so I

picked her up to put her out. The window at the end of the hall opens on the fire-escape, and the cats always use that route to get to our floor. When I opened the window and dumped Charity out, I decided to climb out, too. I hadn't done that for a long time, but when I was younger I had used the fire escape landing a lot. It was one of my favorite places to sit with my guitar and make up songs and sing them. It's on the south side of the house, sheltered from the wind, and on sunny days it can be warm there even in the midst of winter. The trapped sunlight warms your skin, but the thin air stays as cold as ever in your lungs. If you stay too long the air wins out, but for a little while it feels wonderful.

Charity had started down the fire escape, but when she looked back and saw me, she came right back up and climbed into my lap. I'm not crazy about cats in general and Charity in particular, but she made a good hand warmer so I let her stay. Prudence and Charity are Dad's cats. At least he was the one who brought them home because somebody was about to drown them. They're real nothings, as cats go, scrawny black-striped alley cats, both of them; but at least Prudence has enough originality not have kittens two or three times a year.

Charity was so surprised to have me hold her that she started purring up a storm, and it felt good on my hands, warm and vibrating. I leaned back against the sunwarmed shingles and vegetated. I tried not to think about anything, but in a couple of minutes I was thinking about the job at Wentworth and what it would have been like if Dad had taken it.

First of all, if we had moved it would have meant no more Randolph High. There were a lot of reasons why I would have been glad to see the last of Randolph. I felt then that it was really a lousy place to go to school—unless you happened to be part of the "in" group that ran everything. And if you weren't a part of it, there was nothing much you could do about it. I knew because I'd tried.

A year and a half before, when I had started in at Randolph I'd had high hopes. I'd never felt like I really belonged to a school before—I'd always been a real outcast at Lincoln—but I'd decided that things were going to be different at Randolph. All the time at Lincoln I'd had this vague idea that everybody else, all the other kids, had some kind of secret that I wasn't in on—something that made them able to talk and laugh and kid around together. And I was so sure that I couldn't find out what the secret was I didn't even try. I just did my work and left. But then in the eighth grade I began to see things differently.

I was noticing a lot of things along about then. I began to watch people—I mean, really watch them— and I decided that nearly everyone was afraid, at least a little, and there wasn't any big secret. Only a lot of little ones. One of the little secrets was to dress like everyone else, or just a little bit better. And another was to talk like everyone else and about the same kinds of things. Another one, for a boy, was to be a good athlete. Of course, that was out for me, but I decided there wasn't any reason why I couldn't work on the other things. I knew I was smart—everyone said so and my grades were always good—so why couldn't I learn how to be just like everyone else? Only at Lincoln it was too late to start.

So I concentrated on getting ready for Randolph. I saved money for clothes and practiced remarks and wisecracks that might come in handy. I even dropped out of orchestra because the violin didn't fit my new image. Dad didn't like my quitting, though he didn't try to make me change my mind, but Mr. Cooper, the orchestra teacher, almost had a fit. It was too bad, I guess. But it couldn't be helped.

Then I'd started high school and things weren't anything like I'd planned. Oh, it was better than Lincoln and I made a few friends, but not anything like I'd been counting on. I did get to know this one kid in my English class right away. His name was Jerry Davidson and he was almost as quiet as I was, but he had a good sense of humor when you got to know him. He lived up in Hill Groves and he asked me up to his house a few times. His family had this terrific place with a swimming pool and a rumpus room and the whole bit and they were all very nice and friendly.

I also began to find out that girls thought I was good-looking, but the ones who seemed to like me usually weren't the ones I was interested in—and most of the time I couldn't get up my nerve to talk to any of them, anyway. I still panicked and got tongue-tied at times, particularly around kids I used to know at Lincoln before I started work on the new me. So I'd finally decided that what I needed was a new start. A new start in a school where nobody remembered how I'd been at Lincoln.

For quite a while I'd been thinking that if Dad would just get a job, or even a new batch of students in a part of town where people had enough money to pay a decent fee for their lessons, we could sell the old house and move into a house or apartment in another part of the city. It didn't have to be anything fancy. Just a normal place, instead of a kind of perpetual open house for all the kids and bums and college students and animals in the neighborhood.

So Wentworth would have been the answer. But Dad had turned it down already so that was that. I knew from past experience there was no use discussing it with him any further. It all had to do with a difference in the way we looked at things that was absolutely basic.

My dad's life is the kind of life he picked out for himself a long time ago, and it suits him fine. His mother's family had a lot of money at one time and Dad was brought up in a very strict and proper home with all sorts of rules and regulations. So, when he was still pretty young he ran away from home and lived in

Paris for several years with a lot of artists and writers and types like that. Then when his money was gone and he had to come back home, he just brought his Paris way of living back to Cathedral Street. By renting part of the house and teaching a little, he made enough money to get by and the rest of the time he spends "living" as he calls it. He composes some and plays a little—accompanying and with chamber orchestras—and he goes to all the cheap musical events at the university and to standing room at the opera and symphony. Besides that he reads a lot and spends time with his thousand and one friends—and then there's the mountains. He has this thing about the wilderness, and every few months he takes off with a friend or two and they back-pack into the mountains for a week or so. I've gone with him a time or two, but I'm not much of a hiker because of my leg, so usually I stay home with whoever happens to be living here at the time.

It's a great life I suppose—a lot of people say so. Phil and Dunc and their friends are always raving about how Dad is one guy who dropped out of the rat-race and made it stick. I don't argue with them. I can't even explain to myself exactly how I feel about it. But I know that day on the fire escape I decided it must be a lot bigger kick to drop out of something than not to be *in* in the first place.

Chapter 7

THE NEXT DAY ON MY WAY HOME FROM SCHOOL I stopped by Alcott-Simpson's again. I was planning on walking right through from the east entrance to the west—just to have a quick look around. At least that's what I had in mind when I went in. Everything seemed quiet, and there was a fairly good-sized crowd of shoppers. If there still seemed to be something not quite normal—well, I thought maybe it was only my imagination. I was almost to the west entrance when somebody touched my arm.

I glanced around, and there was this fantastically sophisticated-looking woman. Since I couldn't imagine what she wanted of me, I decided I must have been in her way, so I said, "Excuse me" and stepped to one side. But then this dame, instead of breezing on by, put her arm through mine and smiled at me. I nearly passed out.

She looked like a model who had just stepped out of one of those really far-out fashion magazines. Her hat was an egg-shaped helmet that completely covered her hair and sloped down to a little slanted brim over her eyes. Her suit was kind of egg-shaped too, and made out of some very heavy material with a thick stand-out collar. She was wearing very short black boots with high heels and some huge wrap-around dark glasses that covered more than half her face. Everything she was wearing positively reeked of money, but like most of those high-style things, the whole effect was just a small—but important—inch away from being ugly. But there was one thing you could really say about it, it made a great disguise. Until she started to talk, I hadn't the slightest idea who she was.

"Don't you know who I am?" was the first thing she said.

I started to laugh. The minute she opened her mouth, it ruined the whole effect. All of a sudden it was like some little girl dressed up in her mother's clothes.

"I didn't even know you," I said.

"Do you like it?" she asked. She tugged at the helmet where it came down tight and flat against her cheeks. She sounded worried.

"Like it? You look like something from another planet."

She turned around and looked at herself in a mirror on the counter. "Another planet?" she said thoughtfully. "I saw a model wearing it, and I thought it would make me look different. So no one would know me. But you don't like it?"

"It's fantastic," I said. "You look better than most people would in it."

She smiled again and took hold of my arm. "Let's go to the Tea Room and eat something."

That shook me a little. I'd never taken a girl anywhere to eat anything before, for one thing. And for another, I didn't have a whole lot of money along. At the Alcott-Simpson Tea Room, even a milk shake isn't exactly cheap. I didn't have the slightest idea what I'd do if she ordered a whole lot of stuff. And she certainly might. A teen-age girl who could afford to buy an outfit that probably cost several hundred dollars, just because she wanted to look different, probably wouldn't think anything of ordering everything on the Tea Room menu. Of course, there was the other possibility—that the outfit was stolen, and Sara was a thief, a shoplifter. But that didn't make my problem any better. It wouldn't be any easier to predict what a girl who could *steal* an outfit like that would do.

But when we got to the Tea Room, Sara didn't even look at the menu. She just said, "What can we have? I don't have any money. Do you have any?"

I was right in the middle of making feverish plans to keep her from knowing that I wasn't carrying a bank roll, but the way she asked—straight out—surprised me into answering the same way. "Not much," I said. "But we could have a shake or something."

"Could I have one of those?" Sara asked, pointing

to a soda that a waitress was serving. I checked the menu and told her it was okay. I had enough for two sodas.

We didn't talk much at first while we drank our sodas, but I did get a chance to really look at Sara. Of course, I couldn't see her eyes because of the dark glasses, but I could see enough to tell that I had been right about her face, it was really fantastic. Every time she looked up and caught me looking at her she smiled —not a come-on smile or a wise one, at least not as far as I could tell. Just a quick straight unconditional sort of smile, like you might get from a friendly four-year-old. I couldn't begin to figure her out.

After a while I got around to asking some of the questions that I'd been thinking about. For instance, I started out by asking how old she was.

"By the way," I said. "I've been wondering how old you are. It's sort of hard to tell. Sometimes you look lots older than others."

She gave a little laugh. "How old are you?" she asked.

"Almost fifteen," I said.

She just nodded, so I said, "Well?"

"Oh," she said. "I'm—almost the same."

"You mean you're fourteen?"

She puckered her forehead for a minute, and then she smiled and said, "Almost?" But it sounded more like a question than an answer. It wasn't until later that I realized I still wouldn't want to bet on how old she was. That's the way most of the things I asked her seemed to turn out. Like, I mentioned that I'd seen her at Alcott-Simpson's three times lately and asked how come she spent so much time there.

"Oh, it's all right," she said. "I'm supposed to be here."

That made me think maybe I was right when I'd guessed that she was the daughter of some store big shot. That would explain a lot of things. "Do you have relatives here in the store?" I asked.

Sara just looked at me for a minute and then she nodded and said, "Yes. You're here a lot, too. Do you have relatives here, too?"

So I got started trying to explain why I hung around the store so much. It took quite a bit of explaining. I even went into how I had plans to maybe work there someday, after I'd had business training of course, so I could be something besides just a clerk. Then I asked her if she knew anything about the mysterious stuff that had been going on lately, the dogs and special detectives and everything.

Right away she bit her lip and looked away. I couldn't see her eyes behind the dark glasses, but I had the feeling that she didn't want to answer. She poked at her soda with her straw, and then she sighed and shook her head. "Things have happened—accidents. Most of the time it was just an accident."

"What kind of things?"

"Oh, things get broken. And noises. There have

been noises."

"What do you mean noises?"

"Oh, just laughing and talking. Some of the clerks say they've heard laughing and talking." Sara shook her head and pulled her lips down as if she were disapproving.

"Laughing and talking?" I said. "Why would that bother anyone? I'm talking about whatever it is that made them hire all the extra detectives and dogs. That scream for instance, the other day. Do you know what the screaming was about?"

Sara started playing with her straw again, and I could tell she didn't want to answer, but after I'd asked her again about the scream she finally said, "Yes, I know. There was a lizard in the dressing room. Just a lizard from the Pet Shop. A big green one."

I started to laugh. It hit me all of a sudden—the picture of some old dame suddenly noticing she was sharing her dressing room with a big green iguana. That would explain the scream all right. "But how did it get there?" I asked. "The Pet Shop is clear down on the first floor."

"Someone forgot to put it away. I don't think they meant to frighten anyone." Sara was leaning towards me and she sounded very serious and kind of apologetic, as if she were worried about what I would think. I wished I could see her eyes. I couldn't help wondering if the whole thing was some kind of a put-on. She sounded so sincere and on the level, but the whole thing didn't quite make sense. The whole conversation seemed to have holes in it, like when you tune in late to a mystery program and miss a bunch of important clues.

"Look," I said, "I'm not sure I know what we're talking about. It doesn't matter to me who put the iguana in the dressing room, and I really don't care whether it was done on purpose or not. But what I would like to know is exactly who you are and what you have to do with the whole thing—and where you get your information. I'm around this store pretty much myself, and usually I hear a lot about what's going on but—"

Just about then Sara stood up suddenly and looked around. "I have to go now," she said; and without even waiting for me to answer, she walked out of the Tea Shop. By the time I'd paid for the sodas, she had disappeared. I looked all over the store but I couldn't find her anywhere.

While I was looking around, it occurred to me that Madame Stregovitch might know something about Sara. In the past I'd found that if there was any interesting gossip going around the store, Madame would be sure to know all about it. I was almost back to Cosmetics before I remembered that it was Madame's day off. There wasn't much else I could do right then, so I started down the Mall towards the west entrance. But somewhere along the way, I drifted into the indoor garden. There was still a quarter of an hour until closing time, and I guess I was thinking that if I waited around there was a chance I might see Sara again.

The indoor garden, or the Garden Court as it was called, was one of the most unusual things about Alcott-Simpson's. It was a large area in the middle of the street floor that looked so much like a real garden you could almost believe it was, unless you looked up and saw the ceiling instead of the sky. The walks were made of something that looked like stone. There were stretches of green carpeting that looked a lot like grass, and dozens of potted shrubs and bushes and even small trees. Here and there there were singing birds in cages and hanging baskets full of fancy flowers like orchids and begonias. The smaller plantings were always being changed to fit the seasons, and at Christmas time it was always made into a winter garden with artificial ice and snow. All through the garden there were little alcoves with benches for shoppers to sit down for a few minutes and catch their breath. Right in the middle of the garden there was a big fountain.

The center part of the fountain was a pyramid of stone cupids and dolphins. The water came out of the dolphins' mouths and arched down into a large pool. Around the pool was a stone wall about two feet high and wide enough to make a comfortable place to sit. It was always a good place to kill a few extra minutes.

I sat down on the stone wall and wiggled my fingers in the water to make the goldfish curious. I hadn't seen anyone near the fountain as I came up, but I'd only

been sitting there for a few minutes when a toy ship came bobbing into sight from the other side of the pyramid. It was a typical Alcott-Simpson toy, a beautiful scale model of an old Spanish galleon, with three masts full of tiny sails, and ropes and rigging in all the right places. For a second I wondered if someone had left it there, but then I realized that it was moving too fast to be only drifting. Someone on the other side of the stone pyramid had given it a push or else blown into its sails, probably some little kid whose mother had just bought it for him on the fourth floor and who couldn't wait until he got home to try it out. I started listening then, and sure enough, in a minute I heard something—little kids' voices whispering right on the other side of the fountain. Because of the noise of the splashing water, I couldn't make out what they were saying; but I thought I could tell that they were giggling a little, as if they thought they were playing a trick on me—maybe making me think the ship was sailing around under its own power. I decided to go along with the gag, so when the ship got clear around to my side I leaned way out, caught it, turned it around and blew it back the way it had come. It went bobbing back around the fountain, and in a minute I heard giggling again, and in another minute it came sailing back. I was waiting for it to come alongside, and thinking that this time I'd pick it up and carry it back to them just to keep the game from getting monotonous, when I heard the closing bell begin to ring. So I left the game unfinished and hurried off to take a last look through the homeward bound crowds. I didn't even think much more about it at the time.

Chapter 8

THAT NIGHT WHILE I WAS TRYING TO TRANSLATE SOME French sentences, I kept thinking about Sara. I'd translate a few words and then just sit there for several minutes staring into space. After a while I began to realize that I was thinking about Sara all the time, even when I was looking up words and practicing pronunciations. I could be right in the middle of some word, with all the old brain cells clicking away normally, but in some strange sort of way, Sara was there, too, like a shadow hovering right there in the back of my mind. I remember that once, right out loud, I said, "Dion, old pal, you've got it bad. You are really *haunted*."

That is the exact word I used—*haunted*. I had a feeling even then that it wasn't just the ordinary boy-girl thing. Of course I wasn't any great authority on the subject, but I'd spent some time thinking about girls before. Who hasn't? I mean, nobody gets to be almost 15 without giving quite a bit of thought to people of the opposite sex. And even though I hadn't had much experience with girls, because of being out of things all those years, I'd had plenty of chances to make observations and get a lot of general information. Among the people who hung around the Val James Combination Music School—Group Therapy Center—and Soup Kitchen, there had always been a certain percentage of females: friends of Dad's, or of our renters, or just friends of friends. And I'd had lots of opportunities to observe the kind of hang-ups that people can get into over a person of the opposite sex. But this was different. I didn't know how or in what way, but I knew this was not the ordinary kind of thing.

When I finally finished my homework, I went into the kitchen for a bedtime snack. Dad was out at one of his musical evenings somewhere, but the college crowd was there as usual. Matt was reading, or trying to, and Phil and Dunc and a friend of theirs named Josh were practicing on their guitars.

Josh was one of the characters who hung around our place a lot, and he and I had never particularly appreciated each other. We get some far-out types around our place, and Josh is one of the farthest. He's supposed to be some sort of expert on the guitar, and that night he was teaching Phil and Dunc some new picks and strums.

Nobody paid any attention to me, which was fine as far as I was concerned, even if it was my kitchen. I looked around for something to eat, but I couldn't find much except dirty dishes. Finally I put some butter and brown sugar on a piece of stale bread and poured myself a glass of milk. I sat down to listen to the guitar lesson while I ate.

Josh was trying to show Phil how to do something that looked a lot like the Travis pick, but it seemed to me that neither one of them really knew what he was doing.

I was thinking of saying something about it when Matt, who had quit trying to read and was listening too said, "Di used to do a pick something like that. Didn't you, Di?"

I nodded. "Something," I said.

Josh rolled his eyes up at me from under his wad of hair without uncurling from around the guitar. "Yeah?" he said. "Like what?"

"Oh, I just had a melody and a rhythm beat going at the same time. But it wasn't quite like that."

"So show us," Josh said, unwrapping himself and sticking his guitar out in my direction, like he thought I was going to drop my bread and leap across the room to take it.

"No thanks," I said. "I gave it up."

"Gave what up?" he said, still holding the guitar out sort of limply.

"The guitar habit. I quit. It takes too much time."

Josh went on looking at me, and then he looked at Phil and Dunc, and then he shrugged and pulled in his arm. He hunched over and began to strum. "Man," he muttered into his beard, "this kid has a problem. What is he—about twelve? And already he's running out of time."

Phil laughed. "Oh, Di's all right. It's just that he's a throwback. A typical member of the younger generation of 1910."

I wasn't sure exactly what he was driving at, but I didn't want to give him the satisfaction of asking; so I went back to my bread and sugar, and in a little while Phil and Dunc and their crummy friend straggled out to go to some coffee shop where a lot of their other friends hung out. So Matt and I were left alone in the kitchen.

It was getting cold and Matt got up and rummaged through the wood box for some more stuff to throw on the fire. There wasn't much left but he managed to stir up a little heat and we both moved closer.

"Is that the straight scoop?" Matt asked. "Have you really quit playing the guitar for good?"

I shrugged. "I don't know. I think so."

"Why?"

"Why not? As far as I can see, this whole music thing is for suckers. There's almost nothing you can do that takes so much time and work, and what do you get out of it? Maybe one guy in a couple of million gets to where he can make any real money with it. Besides, I've got my future all planned and there just isn't going to be much time for music."

"I see," Matt said. Then he just sat there for a long

time fooling with his beard and looking at me in a funny way, like he was half amused and half disgusted. I was already beginning to get mad when he started out. "Well, there's just one thought I'd like to offer. You might very well get to be the one in a couple of million who makes it with music. I'll bet the odds against being born with the kind of musical talent you have are almost that extreme."

I laughed. "Thanks," I said. "But I've been through that stage. Daydreaming about being some big star or concert artist. Fat chance. And besides, I don't have the personality for it. To be a big star, more than half of it is personality—the way you come on. And I just don't have it."

"How do you know you don't?"

"I know. When I went to Lincoln, I used to have to play violin solos with the orchestra." All of a sudden I was remembering those solos—in the bottom of my stomach. Me limping on stage in my outgrown suit and frozen smile, and the guys from my class giggling in the front row. "It made me sick," I said. "I mean sick!"

"Okay. Okay," Matt said. "So you don't want to be a professional musician. You still wouldn't have to quit music altogether. You used to play and sing for hours at a time, with nobody ever twisting your arm or even telling you to practice. And now—nothing. I don't get it."

"I told you. I don't have time anymore," I said. "I

94

have plans, other things to do."

"Yeah, I know," Matt grinned. "Phil was right when he called you a throwback. With half the kids in the country rebelling against the whole scene, here you are knocking yourself out to be a part of it. How come?"

I got up and slammed the milk into the refrigerator and started out of the room. "Di! Di, wait a minute," Matt said.

So I stopped halfway out the door, without turning around. "I'm sorry," Matt said. "I wasn't trying to put you down. I really just want to know. How come?"

"How come!" I said. "How do I know how come? I haven't figured it out. I don't have time. And I can't help it if I'm not rebelling in the right direction. Everybody has to rebel against what he has to rebel against. Not what somebody else has."

Chapter 9

WHEN I GOT TO MY ROOM, I SLAMMED THE DOOR AND
threw myself down on my bed. I lay there for about
thirty seconds and then I sat up and punched my pil-
low, took off my shoes, turned off the light and lay
back down. In about thirty seconds more, I got up
again, turned on the light and put my shoes back on.
I found a book I'd been reading, took it over to my
desk and got out a pencil and ruler to mark important
passages. After I'd read about two sentences, I put the
book down, grabbed my jacket, and left the house.

I didn't have any idea where I was going. I just
felt I had to get out. I hunched my head down inside
my turned-up collar, stuck my hands in my pockets
and started to walk. But I'd only gone a few blocks
when I realized I was heading toward Alcott-Simpson's. I knew it would be closed, but I told myself that
as long as I was walking, there wasn't any reason why
I shouldn't walk in that direction if I felt like it.

It was a strange night. There was a low misty overcast, so thick that in spots it was almost like walking through drifting clouds. There wasn't any wind, though, so after a few fast blocks I didn't feel the cold at all. In what seemed like only a few minutes, I'd reached the corner of Palm and Eighth.

I looked around. The cold mist was thicker than it had been down in our part of town. The street lights were only small fuzzy glares, and José's shuttered-up flower stand was draped in a floating white veil. There was a stillness, as if the city sounds were deadened, drowned in the fog. Except for a car or a scurrying pedestrian appearing and quickly disappearing into the gloom, the city looked deserted, like a land of the dead. I decided to walk around the block once quickly and then go right on home.

All around Alcott-Simpson's the fog was almost like a living thing, clammy cold and dripping; but inside the display windows, the lighting had a golden tone, warm and rich. More than ever it was like looking into a separate world. I walked by windows set up as rooms beautifully furnished, windows full of haughty manikins dressed in the latest styles, and one that was an elaborate ski lodge scene with a bunch of manikins in ski clothes standing around a fireplace with lots of skiing equipment carefully scattered around. When I came to the west entrance, I stopped and peered into the ground floor.

The huge stretch of the main floor of Alcott-Simpson's was almost dark. Dim lights were on in just a few

places, and here and there a pale glow lit a length of gilded pillar or reflected in a mirror or counter top. In between and back behind, the rest of the floor seemed to go on forever, dim and shadowy. It made me think of a huge cave, maybe the treasure cavern in the Arabian Nights with endless riches making golden sparkles in the gloom. I leaned against the fog-wet glass and whispered "Open Sesame" but nothing happened. I went on around the block, and it wasn't until I had stopped again at the east entrance that I saw something moving way back in the shadows.

It was a long way off at first among the potted trees at the edge of the Garden Court and it appeared and then disappeared among the deeper shadows. Two or three times I told myself that I was only imagining it; but then suddenly it was close enough so that I knew I wasn't. I wasn't imagining it, and when she turned into the main aisle that led to the east entrance I could see that it was a girl—a girl wearing a long white dress with dark hair hanging down over her shoulders. Even before she was near enough for me to see her face, I knew it was Sara. When she was quite close, she began to run and in a second she was unlocking the door; I was inside before I had time to think.

The minute I heard the door locking behind me, I wasn't sure I wanted to be inside Alcott-Simpson's again after closing time. The first time had been bad enough. "Hey," I whispered, "what's going on? What are you doing in here? I mean, what are we doing in here?"

For a second she didn't say anything; she just looked at me and smiled that all-out smile, like a little kid on Christmas morning. Then suddenly she looked behind me at the door and said, "Hurry. This way." We ducked back into a side aisle as some people walked by on the sidewalk outside.

We stood there in the shadows waiting for them to get out of sight, and I said, "Look, this is crazy. I don't want to go through this again."

"It's all right," Sara said. "The dogs are gone now. And the guards are all in the watchman's room. I know all about when they come and where they look. They won't see us. If we go upstairs, no one will see us."

I don't know why, but I believed her absolutely. I was sure that she knew what she was talking about; I was sure that the police dogs were gone and that the watchman would only be where she expected them to be and that she was right about us being safe upstairs. But there was one thing I wasn't sure about, and I was thinking about that all the time as Sara led the way through the shadowy aisles and up the escalator. I was wondering *how* she knew and *why* she knew and what part she played in the whole big mystery that had been going on at Alcott-Simpson's.

When we got to the mezzanine, she stopped and waited for me.

"I didn't believe it," she said in a breathless rush.

"When they said you were right outside, I didn't believe it."

For a second I thought I mustn't have heard her right. "When who said?" I gasped. "Who said I was right outside?"

Sara looked startled for a split second, but then she laughed. "Oh just some friends of mine," she said. "I have some other friends in the store."

I looked around. "But who—and where are they? I haven't seen anyone except you—and the guards that time. Is that it? Are the guards your friends?"

She laughed. "Oh no. The guards aren't my friends. My friends are—they're here someplace, in the store. It's a very big store."

"It's a very big store," I said in a sarcastic tone of voice. "Well, thanks for the news. Now look. You've said something about other people, other people in the store, before. I want to know what you're talking about. I want to know what I'm getting into. These friends of yours, are they people who work here or are they—the ones the guards have been hired to catch? The ones who've been stealing things. I'm not going to rat on anybody, but I don't want to get mixed up in——"

I faded out about then because all of a sudden I noticed that Sara was—well, not crying exactly, but her eyes had an underwater look and her chin was moving. It shook me up. I'd never seen a girl cry before, except a few real little ones, and I'd sure as hell never *made* a girl cry before. I don't remember exactly what I said next, but I do know I stopped asking questions. I just began talking and I kept on until she smiled again, and when I was through I knew I'd said things I hadn't meant, or at least I hadn't meant them until I said them. I'd said that it didn't matter to me who the others were and it didn't matter what they were doing in Alcott-Simpson's and that I wouldn't ask her about them any more. She looked up at me then and smiled, and her eyes were fantastic. For just a minute I felt my skin prickle all over the way it does when music is beautiful beyond any sort of reason or expectation.

"Let's go up to the second floor," she said, and her voice sounded normal and cheerful. "I left some things up there, and I have to put some dresses away."

So we went on up to the second floor and walked way back through the women's clothing departments to where evening dresses and coats were sold. Near some tall three-sided mirrors there was a chair piled high with evening dresses. Sara began putting the dresses on hangers and putting them away. "I was looking at them," she explained. "But I always put things away when I've finished." One of the dresses she put away was very much like the one she was wearing, long and white and floaty. I wondered if she'd just borrowed it off the rack, too.

On another chair near the mirrors was a bouquet of flowers, some kind of very small orchids—golden tan flecked with brown. When Sara finished putting away the dresses, she picked up the flowers. "I got these downstairs," she said. "Would you like one?" She gave me an orchid, and I put it in the buttonhole of my jacket. Sara stood in front of the mirror and put the others in her hair—crisp dark gold against soft black.

"What do you want to see?" she asked then.

"I don't care," I said.

"All right," she said, "I think I'd like a necklace. Shall we go find me a necklace?" I guess I looked worried at that because she added, "It's all right. I'll put it back after a while."

I was afraid she meant to go back down to the Gem Shop on the first floor where there were real diamonds and other jewelry that cost an awful lot of money. I didn't much like the idea of fooling around with that sort of thing, even if she did mean to put it back. But it turned out that she was only heading for a costume jewelry counter on the second floor. When we got there, she took all kinds of things out of the cases and tried them on—earrings, necklaces, bracelets. She kept asking me what I thought about each one, but they all looked okay to me and I said so. At last she put everything back except a long string of green beads and a heavy medallion of some kind of metal. After she put them on she said, "Where shall we go now?"

"I don't know," I said, but then I had an idea. "I always used to have dreams about having the Alcott-Simpson's toy department all to myself. It might be fun to see what it's like—just for old time's sake."

Sara paused for a minute, and I thought she looked uncertain, maybe even worried, but then she nodded. "All right, let's go to the toy department."

So we started on up to the fourth floor, but not very directly. Walking with Sara was not like walking with anyone else. We moved in the same direction but not in the same way or at the same rate of speed. I walked slowly, trying hard not to make any noise, straining my ears and eyes against the unaccustomed silence and shadows. And all the time Sara came and went around me so that it was almost like walking with an unleashed puppy. She kept going and coming—skipping ahead and running back—telling me to come see something or else bringing something back to me. Once she was gone for a second and came back with a big hat made of pink ostrich feathers. "Isn't it beautiful—so beautiful," she said, holding it out for me to touch. She put it on her head and pulled the feathery brim down around her face and laughed and ran back to put it away. We made detours to look at some golden slippers, a manikin in a wedding dress, and some home gym equipment. Sara wanted to touch everything, try it out, and she kept saying that everything was beautiful. After a while I felt a little less nervous, and I tried out a few things, too. I rowed on the rowing machine and rode the stationery bicycle in the gym display, while Sara sat on a balancing horse and watched and laughed. I laughed, too, but I couldn't hold on to the feeling of having a good time. There was a kind of frustration in the strangeness of the situation that kept bothering me, when Sara was out of sight, and other times, too. The other times were now and then when Sara would stop and a shadow would pass over her face, like a memory of something terrible and hopeless.

We had just gotten to the top of the escalator at the fourth floor when Sara stopped and stood for a second as if she were listening. "Wait," she said. "Wait here a minute. I'll be right back."

"Why?" I asked. "Where are you going?"

Sara motioned to the left where you could see the top of the arch that led to the toy department. "There," she said. "To see if everything is all right. I'll be right back. Stay here until I come back. Please stay here."

"But—but," I said, and I was still protesting when she ran away. I hadn't really promised, and I had almost decided to follow her anyway when she came running back.

"No," she said. "Let's not go there now. We'll go there later. Let's go back downstairs now."

She started back down the escalator, and I followed after her feeling stranger than ever. Like having the kind of dream where crazy unexplainable things keep happening and you realize it's crazy but you can't wake up and make it stop.

When we got back to the ground floor, we went to

the left around the Mall. I tried to question Sara about the toy department and why we couldn't go there, but she only shook her head. Except for that, she seemed the same as before, laughing and talking and rushing around. We stopped for a while in the Music Shop. There were a lot of guitars in some big glass cabinets and I mentioned to Sara that I played. Right away she wanted me to play one. "Sure," I said. "That's all we need to bring every guard in the place down on our necks."

"Oh no," Sara said. "It's all right. The guards don't go on their rounds very often anymore. They have a place down in the basement where they all stay together. They won't hear."

If I'd really stopped to think about it, I would have realized that that didn't make much sense, but at that point I was ready to believe just about anything Sara said. I was starting to see if I could get a guitar out of the cabinet when all of a sudden I heard voices. I froze on the spot, listening. In a minute I could tell that I wasn't hearing loud voices still a long way off, but very soft voices coming from someplace very near. My heart went limp for a second and then caught up with a huge thudding rush. I reached for Sara's hand to pull her away, but she dodged away from me and stood still, listening.

"Come on," I barely breathed. "Let's get out of here."

She shook her head. "Stay here," she said. "I have

to find out. I'll be right back."

She moved in the direction of the voices, and after a minute I followed. By the time she got to the arch that led into the next department, I was only a few steps behind. We went around the corner—and then I started to laugh. We were in the TV shop and all it was was a big color TV set that had been left on by some careless clerk.

I began laughing like crazy; it really wasn't that funny but I was feeling dizzy with relief. Then all at once I noticed Sara's face. She wasn't laughing, and she looked hard at the TV and then very quickly all around the shop as if she were looking for something. She was frowning a little and pressing her lips together hard.

"What's the matter?" I said. "It's nothing to worry about. Some dumb clerk just forgot to turn it off." Sara nodded, but she didn't say anything, and she looked back over her shoulder again uneasily.

I remember that it was some old movie that was showing on the TV, one of those old musicals with mobs of dancers in fancy costumes. I walked over to it and gave the knob a big whack and shut it off. "There!" I said, with a big phony self-confident grin. "That takes care of that. I press the magic button and —Presto! No more mysterious voices."

Sara smiled back, only it wasn't a real smile; actually the way she looked at me was almost like an apology. It made me feel confused and stupid and helpless. I had an urge to yell or hit something, but all I did was whisper, "For cripes sake will you tell me what's going on?"

But she didn't. I mean she didn't tell me anything. Instead she walked on slowly, and I followed. We went back around to the east entrance, and Sara opened the door and I went out. The fog was even thicker, and the city seemed, more than ever, like the end of the world.

I was outside before either of us said anything at all. Then Sara said, "Will you come back again?" I nodded and she closed the door and locked it. I watched her walking back towards the escalators with the night lights gleaming and then fading on her white dress until she disappeared in the darkness.

It wasn't until I was home in bed going over everything in my mind that I realized the voices hadn't come from the TV set at all. We'd stood right there in front of the set for at least a minute before I turned it off, and it hadn't made the slightest noise. The sound must have been turned off the whole time.

Chapter 10

Maybe alone on the elevator
A chattering gasp was heard,
Or a pattering rush on the escalator,
Or perhaps it first occurred
As a brush of fingers against the cages,
Of the pet shop's golden birds,
They heard, they sensed, they almost faced it,
And they said it was absurd.

IT WAS THINKING ABOUT THE VOICES AND THE SILENT TV set that gave me the idea for the first verse, because that's the way it was with me. I sensed something that night that I didn't let myself even think about for a long time afterwards because it seemed so crazy. Oh, I thought about what had happened all right, but mostly to figure out some logical explanation.

I lay awake for a long time after I finally got home that night going over and over the whole thing in my mind. It occurred to me that there was a chance something had gone wrong with the sound part of the reception just as we came up—right after I heard the voices. But I knew it wasn't too likely because the sound is usually the last part to go out when there is reception trouble; and if something does go wrong with it, it's more apt to turn into static than into complete silence. Besides, there was the strange way Sara had acted. Finally there didn't seem to be any other explanation: there really were people who were able to get into the store at night—and Sara *did* have something to do with them.

The way I figured it out, Sara must have had some connection with somebody important in the store. Like maybe, her father was one of the owners or executives. That way she would have been able to hang around enough to get hold of some keys and a lot of information about schedules and things like that. And then maybe, she just got started letting other people into the store. Maybe just other kids now and then, like she let me in, or maybe there was a regular gang of some sort. If there was a gang, I was pretty sure it was made up of kids. I don't know why exactly, except that Sara was so young, and also because of things I'd heard. Like, Madame Stregovitch had said that there had only been a little stealing, and Sara herself had said something about accidents and tricks being played. It all sounded like kid stuff.

So I made up a theory, a long complicated one,

about how Sara was a lonely rich kid who didn't have many friends, and who thought up the Alcott-Simpson business as a way to meet people and have something exciting to do. It occurred to me that if she met somebody she really liked, maybe she'd lose interest in letting all the others in before they all got caught and got into serious trouble. I remembered that Sara had said that the dogs weren't being used anymore and that the guards didn't go on their rounds so often, so maybe she'd already stopped letting most of the others in, probably the ones who'd caused the trouble. Only I wasn't just one of the others, because Sara had asked me if I would come back, and I had said yes.

After a while I got too sleepy for long complicated theories, but I went on thinking about Sara clear up until I went to sleep; and even afterward—because I dreamed a lot of crazy stuff that night, and Sara kept drifting in and out of the dream. It was one of those long mixed-up dreams where all sorts of crazy things keep happening, and when I woke up I could only remember bits and pieces of it here and there. But there was one part about me riding this fantastic black horse with a silver mane and tail. I was riding it right down the middle of the street and all the cars were stopping and honking, and then I was riding it up the stairs in the main building at Randolph High. The stairs kept getting longer and longer and wider and wider, and a lot of the kids I know at Randolph were running up the stairs trying to keep up with me on the black horse, and I was laughing and waving back at them. And then all of a sudden the horse started to grow, and he got bigger and bigger until I was like some little monkey clinging to his back, and he began to kick and jump and plunge around. Then I was lying on the ground, and the horse was standing over me as big as a house; and way up on his back I saw Sara, and she was leaning over and reaching down as if she were trying to help me. I could see her as plain as day. She had on the same white dress she'd worn that night at the store, and the wind was whipping her hair across her face so that all I could see was her eyes and they were full of tears the way they'd been when I'd tried to make her explain everything.

When I woke up the next morning, the fog was all gone and it was a bright, sunny day. Everything seemed different. All the things that had happened at Alcott-Simpson's, particularly all the strange unexplainable things, seemed faded and indistinct and sort of a part of the dream I had just been having. During the next few days it all blended and mixed together until at times I wasn't really sure which things had actually happened and which had been part of the dream. I went to school and to work, but for a day or two I didn't go into Alcott-Simpson's at all. I wanted to see Sara again very much, but I didn't want to be in Alcott-Simpson's again at night, and I had a feeling that if I saw Sara again I wouldn't have much choice. Two or three times I walked all around the Alcott-

Simpson block, but I didn't go inside. Not even to get warm, in spite of the fact that it had turned foggy again and very cold.

Once I stopped for a while to talk to José. "Hi, José," I said. "What's new? Seen any more police dogs lately?"

"No, no dogs," José said. "Them dog men geeve up and go away long time ago."

"Gave up?" I asked.

"Sure. Dogs don' do no good. Them dogs go in there and they jus' lie down and cry."

"Lie down and cry?" I said. "What makes them do that? I thought those dogs were supposed to be great at patrolling stores and places like that."

José just shrugged and rolled up his eyes in a way that meant it was too much for him to explain. I stepped inside his booth to get warm by the little foot-warmer stove that he kept there. I bent over it and warmed my hands. "This is the coldest fog I've ever seen," I said.

José nodded. "Spirit-fog," he said.

"What?" I said.

"You know my friend Luke?" José asked.

I nodded. Luke was an old man who had been a janitor at Alcott-Simpson's for years and years. He was a good friend of José's, and he used to come over to the stand during his breaks, just to pass the time of day.

"Luke tell me about theese spirit-fog," José said.

"Back where Luke come from in the big hill country, they have theese theengs."

"What things?"

"Theese fog, that comes white and cold in the place where the spirit leeves, een a low and lonely place between the tall hills. And Luke say that sometimes a man go into theese fog—and he not come out."

"Yeah," I said. "I've heard some of Luke's ghost stories before. He has a million of them. It's just superstition. I'll bet he doesn't really believe all that stuff he tells himself."

"Maybe not," José said. "Maybe not."

I had heard Lukes's stories before, and I'd never paid much attention to them; but that night I was glad when the fog began to thin a few blocks from Alcott-Simpson's. By the time I got home it was practically gone.

Right about then if anyone had asked me if I'd ever go back in Alcott-Simpson's again after hours—that is, if I ever had the chance, and it wasn't likely I ever would—I'd have told them that wild horses couldn't drag me. But that very night I did a funny thing. After I'd finished my homework, I got my guitar down off the wall and began to practice. I didn't decide to do it, I just did it. And while I was practicing I caught myself several times thinking of something to play in terms of what Sara might like to hear. I told myself I was really stupid, but the thought kept coming back. Anyway, regardless of what I was practicing for, I had to admit that it felt great to play again. It had been months since I'd even touched the guitar and I was very rusty, but actually I was surprised how quickly my fingers loosened up and it all began to come back.

The next Saturday was a calm clear day with a softness in the air that almost felt like spring. On my way to Palm Avenue to do my regular Saturday morning jobs, I walked past Alcott-Simpson's and everything looked bright and normal. The morning sun sparkled off its hundreds of windows and lightened the gray of its stone walls. I decided that as soon as I'd finished my work, I'd drop by for a quick visit. If Sara was still hanging around the store, she'd probably be wondering where I'd been. While I swept out at the travel bureau and washed display cases at the stationers store, I was thinking over my "poor little rich kid" theory about Sara, wondering where she lived and what her life had been like to make her so—well, strange really, or at least different.

But when I stopped by Alcott-Simpson's on my way home, I couldn't find Sara anywhere. The store wasn't at all crowded, so it shouldn't have been difficult to find someone; but I didn't see Sara anywhere. As a matter of fact, for a nice warm Saturday, Alcott-Simpson's was amazingly empty; but then, I told myself, maybe it was only because a lot of the customers had taken advantage of the good weather to get out of town for the weekend. Anyway, I looked around pretty thoroughly and I didn't see anyone I knew very well. I even dropped by Madame Stregovitch's counter, but there was a different clerk on duty—someone I'd never seen before. I tried asking her some questions, but she seemed nervous and snappy. She said she didn't know anything at all. She didn't know for sure, but she thought that Madame Stregovitch had been ill. "But I'm not sure," she said. "I haven't been sure about anything at all, lately."

That night right after dinner I went to my room. I knew what I had in mind when I changed my clothes and put my guitar in its plastic case, but I didn't stop to think about it very much. I moved quickly, as if I had an appointment to keep. When I was all ready, I dropped by the kitchen to tell Dad I was going out.

Dad wasn't in the kitchen, but nearly everyone else in the neighborhood was. Phil and Dunc and a couple of their girl friends were sitting around the fireplace arguing about where they ought to go to spend the evening. As usual the problem seemed to be that nobody had any money. The youngest Grover kid was crawling along on the floor, dragging a dishtowel and watching Charity, who was hiding behind a chair leg and getting ready to pounce out as the dishtowel went by. Matt and Mr. Rosen, an old chess friend of Dad's from up the street, had the chess board out on the kitchen table.

I took the dishtowel away from the kid and made a werewolf snarl at him; he rolled over on his back like a puppy coaxing to be played with. Charity must have thought I wanted to play, too, because she danced out sideways from under the chair and grabbed me by the ankle. But I didn't have any time to play. I shook Charity loose and asked loudly if anyone happened to know where my dad was. Everybody looked up blankly, like they couldn't remember who I was for a minute. "My Dad?" I repeated, "you know, the guy who lives here?"

"Oh yeah, him," Phil said. "He retired to his studio just a minute ago—" he stopped and fluttered his eyebrows "—with a charmer from the P.T.A."

It might have taken me a minute to figure out what he was talking about, except that just then I heard the piano and, a second later, a horrible screeching soprano with a vibrato like an excited turkey. "Ohhh-say can you seeeeee?" the voice warbled. I knew, then, what was going on. Dad had told me about this dame who'd been over a couple of times to practice her singing. She was the mother of one of his piano students, and she imagined herself to be a singer. Somehow she'd talked the P.T.A. she belonged to into asking her to lead the National Anthem at their next meeting. Of course she wasn't paying Dad anything for coaching her. She was just "dropping by a couple of times to warm up with a piano." Dad told me about it as if it were kind of a joke on him, but I had an idea that it was one charity he regretted. That kind of a voice would be like scraping chalk on a blackboard as far as

Dad was concerned.

When I opened the door to the studio, the P. T. A. prima donna unclasped her hands and drifted to a stop in the midst of "the perilous night." Dad turned around from the piano looking so grateful for the interruption that for a minute I felt sorry for him, even if he had brought it on himself.

"Uh, excuse me," I said. "Dad, Jerry Davidson wants me to give him a lesson on the guitar. I won't be back until late." It didn't happen to be a lie. Both statements were true. They just didn't have anything to do with each other. Dad looked at the guitar case and for a second his eyes crinkled up with pleasure. Then suddenly he cooled it and said, "I see. Well, I guess that will be all right," in a carefully indifferent tone of voice. It was easy to see that he was trying not to show that he was happy to see me doing something with music again. It was a perfectly obvious put-on; he never was any good at pretending.

I was on my way down the stairs before it occurred to me what his problem was. He was probably thinking that if he approved of something, I'd quit wanting to do it. I had to admit to myself that it had worked that way at times lately. But I didn't know he knew it.

Chapter 11

IT WAS DARK WHEN I GOT TO ALCOTT-SIMPSON'S, BUT it wasn't foggy and there were a lot more people on the streets than there had been the last time I'd been there at night. I walked around the block, stopping for a few minutes at each entrance. Inside everything looked the same as it had before, dim lights and white-draped counters. I went back around and stopped again at each entrance, but all it got me was some suspicious stares from passers-by. Finally I admitted to myself that it was pretty stupid to think that I could get in that way again—at least, not unless I let Sara know I was coming. She might not be there; she might be there but not know I was outside; or she might even know and be afraid to open the door because of there being so many people on the sidewalks. It had just been a coincidence the time before.

I knew it would look strange if I went home so early, and it occurred to me that I might do what I'd pretended I was going to do. So I called Jerry from a pay phone, and luckily he was at home. When he heard that I was on my way over with my guitar, he got very enthusiastic. I'd given him a couple of lessons when I first got to know him, before I decided to quit music for good, and he'd been after me for a long time to teach him some more.

So instead of seeing Sara that night, I sat around and played the guitar at Jerry's house. Actually it turned out to be not a bad evening. We ate a lot of food that Jerry's mother fixed for us, and Jerry called up another friend of his who wanted to start on the guitar. This guy, whose name is Brett Atwood, came over and I showed them some chords and strums, and the three of us worked out a couple of new arrangements for some old songs. It turned out that Brett had a great voice and he even knew something about music, so together we came up with some pretty good ideas.

After we'd been fooling around for quite a while, I decided to play some of the things I'd written. It was the first time I'd done any of my own stuff for anyone except my dad and some of the people around home; but everything seemed to be going so well that I decided to try it. I was really surprised at the reaction I got. Actually, they made such a fuss I was a little embarrassed. I mean, they really knocked themselves out. Like for instance, Brett—who is a much more swinging type than either Jerry or me—said, "Jerry, Baby, you have really been holding out on me. You said he was good, but you didn't tell me the cat had a bad case of genius."

Afterwards I took the bus home, and when I got off downtown to transfer I walked by Alcott-Simpson's again. It was late by then, and everything in the area was closed up tight. Almost all the pedestrian traffic had stopped and the fog was rolling in, drifting down into the canyons between the tall buildings. Inside Alcott-Simpson's, everything seemed just the same as before. But I waited for a while, and all at once I thought I saw something move way back near the escalator. It was so dark back there it was hard to be sure, but then I thought I saw it again on the same spot. It wasn't coming closer or going away; it was as if someone was just standing there watching. I waited, straining my eyes to see, and whatever it was waited, too. Then a police car drove by slowly, and the cop stared at me so I had to move on. A bus was rolling up to the corner, so I hurried and caught it and went on home. By the time the bus had arrived at our stop I'd figured it out, and gone back to thinking about the evening at Jerry's. What I'd decided was that I'd only been watching a dust sheet draped over something way back in shadows. I'd only imagined I'd seen it move.

That was on Saturday. It was the next Monday morning at the hat shop that I talked to the clerk named Myrna. Myrna had been a clerk in the Pet Shop at Alcott-Simpson's for a year or so. She was a good friend of Jayne Anne, who owned the hat shop where

I worked every Monday morning. She was fairly young and very pale and nervous looking, so that she always made me think of the white mice that were sold in the department where she worked. Now and then, on her way to work in the mornings, Myrna would drop by the hat shop for a quick cup of coffee and a little gossip with Jayne Anne. At the hat shop she was always friendly to me, but if I saw her in Alcott-Simpson's she was very formal because she was afraid of the man who was the department manager. That morning when I got to the hat shop, Jayne Anne was late; the shop was still locked, and Myrna was having hysterics in the alcove outside the front door.

"Dion," she sobbed when I came up, "I'm so glad to see you." She rubbed her eyes with a handkerchief that looked sopping wet already. "Where on earth is Jayne Anne?"

"I don't know. I guess she's a little late. She's this late lots of times on Monday mornings. She'll probably be here any minute."

Myrna wiped her eyes again and looked at her watch. "Oh, I guess it isn't so very late. It just seems like I've been waiting here for—ee—ev—ver." And she broke down and started to cry again.

I felt very uncomfortable. It seemed as if I ought to do something, but I couldn't think what. Finally I said, "Is there anything I could do?" It occurred to me that maybe someone had been chasing her, but there didn't seem to be anyone around. Besides she wasn't the kind of girl that anyone would want to chase, unless it was just to see her run. "Could I call the police, or something?" I said.

"Oh, no-o-o," Myrna said, pulling herself together a little, "no thank you. I'll just wait here and talk to Jayne Anne when she comes. Not that she can help me either, but I just have to talk to someone or I'm going to go crazy." And then she added in a kind of a wail, "if I haven't already."

It occurred to me that if what she needed was someone to talk to, I'd be glad to oblige. I didn't want to see her go crazy and, besides, I was curious. To start things out I ventured a guess. "Did you get fired, or something like that?" I'd heard that the manager of the Pet Shop was a real tyrant.

"Fired?" she said. "Oh, no. Oh, my no. I'm almost the only full time clerk Mr. Braunstetter has left. He couldn't fire me, though I suppose he'll try to blame it on me. He always tries to blame it on one of us. But he couldn't fire me." She stopped and looked at me, and I could tell she was trying to decide how much she should say. I tried to look mature and helpful. She took a deep breath and started out, and once she began it was like a break in the dam. She never even stopped to take a real breath.

"It was this morning—I don't mean that what happened this morning is all of it, because it's been going on for weeks and weeks, but this morning was the last straw. It was my turn to get to work early to clean the cages and do the feeding, so I got there just as the morning janitorial crew was going in. And when we got in, the canaries and parakeets and mynas were loose and flying all over the store. They're catching them now—running all over the store with nets and ladders—but I just couldn't stand it. I couldn't stand it anymore—I just had to get out of there. I didn't even stop to check out."

Myrna had been looking scared to death all along, but when she said that she looked horrified. She was the type who wouldn't be caught dead breaking even the littlest rule, and checking in and out was almost sacred at Alcott-Simpson's. "*I didn't even stop to check out,*" she said again, "*I am going crazy—I'm sure of it.*"

"You said it had been going on for weeks and weeks," I said. "What has? Have the birds been out before?"

"No, not the birds, but other things. Some of the mice, and the kittens—the kittens so many times that we had to stop stocking them. And the chipmunks—and, oh yes, once an iguana. But that's not all. They feed things, too. Right in the middle of the afternoon They feed things. So that you look in the feed trays one minute and they're empty, and the next minute they're full. And They put things in places they shouldn't be—spools of thread in the kittens' cages—wind up toy submarines in the fish tanks—"

"They?" I asked.

"Yes. They!" she said angrily, as if I'd meant I didn't believe her. "Don't take my word for it. It's not just me. It's not just in the Pet Shop either." Her voice got higher and more hysterical. "Oh, a lot of them won't talk about it, because they're afraid of what you'll think, or because they're afraid they'll think it themselves. But if you pick the right ones, the ones who *have* to talk to someone and who can see that you're as scared as they are, they'll tell you. They'll tell you about the sounds They make—feet running and laughter, and voices—and the things that move by themselves—toys, balls that bounce by themselves—and things you see—in dark corners——" She pressed her hands over her mouth as if she were trying to make herself stop.

I felt paralyzed. I opened my mouth to say something, but nothing came out. Just then Jayne Anne came around the corner. "Hello, Di," she said, "sorry to be so late. Myrna! What is it? What on earth is wrong?" She unlocked the door and led Myrna inside, patting her and making sympathetic noises. She stuck her head back out long enough to say, "Di, run along, won't you please. We'll skip the sweeping up for today. Catch me later in the week if you have time." She nodded towards Myrna and made a face that said, "You see how it is."

"Sure," I said. "See you later." And I started off down the sidewalk toward my next job in the Mc-Adam building.

I finished the rest of my Monday morning work in a kind of daze. My mind was just treading water, doing the same things over and over without getting anywhere. The only positive conclusion that I came up with was that I was going to have to see Sara again right away. I was going to have to break my promise about not asking any questions. For my sake, and maybe for her own too, Sara was going to *have* to tell me what she knew about whatever it was that was going on at Alcott-Simpson's.

Chapter 12

Maybe they've heard in the toy department
The endless whispered sighs,
Or have they seen on the goosedown couches,
Where each night something lies?
Could they be learning to shun the shadows
For fear of great dark eyes?
They know, they fear, they're almost certain
But they tell each other lies.

REMEMBERING ABOUT POOR MYRNA GAVE ME THE idea for the second verse.

I finished my work in a hurry on that Monday morning, and on my way to catch the bus to school I walked back past Alcott-Simpson's. Through the doors I could see that a few more clerks had arrived. The birds must have all been caught, because I didn't see any ladders or butterfly nets. That is, if there had been any birds; I'd almost decided that poor Myrna was right about going crazy.

But whether there was anything to Myrna's story or not, I was getting more and more frantic about seeing Sara. I almost decided to wait around until nine-thirty so I could take a quick look for Sara before I went to school. I would have, too, even though I hated being late, but I was almost positive she wouldn't be there. No matter what kind of weird home life she had, she probably had to be in school on Monday mornings like everyone else. So I went on to school and tried to keep my mind off the whole thing until I'd had a chance to get some more information. But that afternoon I was back at Alcott-Simpson's as quickly as I could get there after school.

Sara wasn't in the store that afternoon either. I hung around until the closing bell rang, and she just wasn't there. The crowds were very light again, so I was fairly sure that I'd have seen her if she were anywhere around. There weren't many customers, and there didn't seem to be as many clerks as usual. I glanced in the pet shop and it seemed quiet and normal enough. Except that Mr. Braunstetter, the department manager, was waiting on customers himself, which was something I'd never seen him do before.

I was on my way home, just a couple of blocks from Cathedral Street, when I passed a bus stop and there was Madame Stregovitch getting off the bus. She was carrying a couple of big packages, so I hurried and caught up with her and asked if I could help her carry something.

"Dion," she said. "How nice to see you. You appear like magic and in the nick of time. My arms are very tired." She gave me the biggest package, and we started off down Willow Street. I'd been wanting another chance to question Madame about the trouble at Alcott-Simpson's, and this seemed like a made-to-order opportunity. But I remembered that the last time I'd tried, she'd seemed pretty reluctant to give any answers. So I thought I'd ease into the subject as carefully as I could. I began by saying that I'd heard she'd been sick and I hoped she was okay now. She said yes, she had been and that she was better. Then, just as I'd gotten around to asking if she thought the store was still having as much trouble, she turned into a driveway.

I had known for years that Madame Stregovitch lived somewhere in the Cathedral Street neighborhood, because I used to see her around now and then, but I'd never known exactly where. The driveway we were walking down led back behind an old Victorian town house that had been turned into apartments years and years before. It was a mess of peeling paint, cracked windows and crumbling ornaments—the kind of thing that artists and tourists love, but nobody in their right mind would want to live in. But Madame didn't go into the big house. We went around back and behind the garage we came to a gate that led into a tangled overgrown mess of trees and bushes that had probably once been a garden. Almost hidden in the bushes was a small house. The little house was probably built at the same time as the big one in front of it, maybe for servants to live in; but now it was fenced off into what looked like a little world of its own. It was old and a little shabby, but not rundown and uncared for like the big house; and sitting there almost hidden in the undergrowth, it gave you a funny feeling. Like you'd stumbled onto a place where time had stopped a long time ago.

Madame Stregovitch unlocked a heavy front door with a small oval window, and we went inside.

"I'll just put these things away," she said taking the packages. "And in the meantime you can get the fire going in the fireplace. Then we'll have a nice cup of tea."

I don't spend much time having tea with old ladies as a rule, but I was curious, and besides I hadn't had a chance yet to ask the questions I'd been planning. The logs were all arranged in the fireplace, so I found some matches on the mantle and got the fire started. Somewhere not far away I could hear Madame bustling around running water and clinking dishes.

When I was putting the matches back, I noticed a bunch of pictures on the mantle—mostly big framed photographs of foreign-looking people. There was one picture I noticed especially. It was larger than the others and in a very fancy frame. It was just a photograph, an old dim photograph of a woman, but there was something about it that made me keep staring at it. She had a kind of shawl draped over her head, and her face looked a little like Madame Stregovitch, dark and bony. But it was mostly the eyes I kept looking at. I've seen pictures before that had eyes that seemed to follow you, but these did more than that. They made you feel like squirming.

The fire was going pretty well and Madame S. still hadn't come back, so I turned away from the picture and walked around the room. It was a small darkish room, stuffed with lots of big old-fashioned furniture and smothered with heavy drapes and curtains. The few places the walls did show, they were covered with pictures, some of them painted or sewn on heavy cloth. In two corners of the room there were little cupboards full of weird looking what-nots. All the time I was wandering around I kept glancing back at that one picture on the mantle, and finally I went back to look at it again. I was standing in front of it when Madame finally came back into the room. She was carrying a tray with a teapot and cups and a plate of little cakes and pastries. She came and stood beside me and looked at the picture, too.

"Who is she?" I asked.

Madame turned away without answering and put the tray on a little table. After a minute she said, "She was my mother."

"I thought she might be," I said. "She looks a little like you."

"Do you think so?" She motioned for me to come

and sit down. "Yes, I suppose it is quite evident. I am quite like her in many ways. It is a likeness I've spent most of a lifetime trying to escape."

"Trying to escape?" I said. I guess I sounded a little surprised. Kids are always running their parents down and nobody pays any attention. But you just don't expect people as old as Madame Stregovitch to do that sort of thing.

"You are shocked," Madame said. "You are thinking perhaps that such an attitude is unsuitable for one of my generation?" I knew she was kind of teasing me, and I got the point. But then she shrugged and said, "Well, perhaps. However, in this case I think you did not understand my meaning. I did not intend to suggest that I disapproved of my mother in the usual manner of younger generations. She was an extraordinary woman, and I did not wish to be like her for an extraordinary reason—I was afraid."

"Afraid?" I said. "Afraid of what?"

But Madame just began pouring tea and saying things like, "Do you take sugar?" and I got the feeling she was wishing she hadn't let the whole conversation get started. I was curious, but I had some other important questions to ask and I didn't want to wear out my welcome before I got around to them. So I went back to the question I had started to ask when we were just getting to the house.

"Well, what do you hear about the trouble at Alcott-Simpson's?" I asked. "Do you think there's been as much—er—excitement lately?"

"Why do you ask? Have you been hearing more rumors?"

"Well, I heard that they weren't using the dogs anymore and not so many extra guards. I was wondering if they've already arrested somebody. Do you know if they've arrested the ones who were causing the trouble?"

Instead of answering me, Madame went off into a long string of the silent chuckles that were her way of laughing. "Hah!" she said finally, "Arrested them. I am afraid not. And as for there being less excitement lately, I had not heard that such was the case. If they are no longer using the dogs, perhaps it is because they proved to be useless. And as for the situation improving—just today one department was closed, perhaps permanently. And there may be others soon."

"Closed?" I said. "I haven't heard anything about that. What did they close?"

Madame looked at me for a moment with a strange expression on her face. "The toy department," she said finally. "Today the toy department was closed. Oh, there was no official announcement, but there are rumors that tomorrow it will be roped off and no clerks will be on duty."

The way Madame was acting puzzled me. I knew that she made fun of Alcott-Simpson's lots of times, particularly the executives and some of the customers. But I didn't think she really hated it or anything.

After all, she'd been making her living there for a long time. But I kept getting the feeling that she was pleased, or at least a little amused by all the trouble.

"But why?" I asked. "Why the toy department?" It gave me a kind of empty feeling. Even though I wasn't hung-up on the Alcott-Simpson toy department the way I once had been, I felt a loss, like when an old dream finally fades away for good. "I mean, the Alcott-Simpson toy department is famous all over the country. It's kind of a symbol for little kids. Even the ones who can't afford to buy anything there."

"Well," Madame said, "the reason being given is that there were economic difficulties—the department was not able to make a profit. But in the past the profits have always been high; for a symbol, the public expects to pay dearly. The real problem seems to have been that the store was no longer able to keep a staff. The clerks in the toy department have been quitting almost as quickly as they have been hired."

"But why?"

Madame shrugged. "Who knows? Many reasons have been given. Who knows which reasons are true ones? Perhaps the real reasons have not yet been given at all. But then, reasons rarely have much to do with reality. Won't you have another pastry, Dion?"

Up to that point I hadn't intended to do much talking myself. I'd only planned to find out what I could from Madame Stregovitch, without going into the rumors I'd heard or any of the things that had happened to me. But something about the way Madame was taking it, making a joke out of it, made me want to force her to admit the seriousness of the whole thing. I guess I was feeling a lot like poor Myrna was when she wanted me to admit that it was more than just a crazy dream.

"Look," I said, "you seem to think this is all very amusing, that there's really nothing to worry about. Well, I know some things—some things I haven't told you. Maybe you'll just laugh them off too, and maybe I hope you do, in a way, but anyway—"

So I started out and told her everything. I began with the rumors I'd heard and the strange little things that had happened: the things José had told me; the way Mrs. Jensen had acted in the toy department; and all about Myrna and the things she had said.

Madame was interested. She watched me closely as I talked, and there was a sharpness to her eyes. But at times her lips still twitched, and her shoulders jerked with amusement. I took a deep breath then and started to tell about Sara. I began at the very beginning—how I'd seen her being chased by Mr. Rogers—and I told it all. How I'd gotten shut in the store the first time. How Sara had let me in again. What Sara had told me about herself, and how she talked about someone she called the Others. About the strange things that had happened when we were together. Long before I was finished, I could see that Madame was finally impressed. Her face had turned as still as stone, but her eyes blazed with interest.

When I had said all that I had to say, Madame leaned towards me. Her voice was harsh and tense, "This child, this Sara, describe her."

"She's not a child," I said, "although, I guess she's not far from it. She's small and dark with huge dark eyes and long black hair."

Madame stood up slowly. She had a strange distant look, as if her eyes were focusing on something far beyond my range of vision. "There is something I must attend to," she said. "Wait here. I won't be long." And she disappeared into the next room.

I waited, wondering uneasily what I'd gotten into. Now that it was done, I wished that I hadn't said so much about Sara. It seemed to me that Madame Stregovitch wasn't at all the kind of person who'd tell on anyone, but you never could be sure. And I knew that, more than anything, I didn't want to be the one to get Sara in trouble. That is, in more trouble than she was already in.

Madame must have been gone for ten or fifteen minutes. When she came back into the room, I hardly knew her. Her face was pale and tired, and her eyes seemed to be set in black holes. She sat down and pulled her chair close to mine.

"Dion," she said, "you must listen carefully and do exactly as I say. You must not go back to Alcott-Simpson's again for a while. Most particularly you must not go back again at night. Perhaps in a few days I may need your help there, at the store, and if I do I will let you know. But until that time, you must *not* go to Alcott-Simpson's again."

"Now wait a minute," I said. "You can't just tell me to do that without explaining why or anything. I have to go back right away. If there is some kind of danger——"

Madame held up her hand to make me stop. "Yes, you are right. You should be told enough to make you understand the importance of what I ask of you." She covered her eyes with her hand and sat perfectly still for so long I was beginning to wonder if she'd gone into some kind of trance. When she finally uncovered her face and began to speak, her voice was high and humming, almost as if she were chanting or reciting from memory. "There are times and places when the usual barriers can be overcome and certain individuals are able to experience the overlapping of divergent forms of existence. This overlapping can take place through many different thresholds and can take many forms. One such form—one such overlapping of worlds —takes place only through a particular threshold, the sleeping or unconscious mind of a child. The mind of a child who is himself at a threshold between two forms of his existence, his childhood and his adult life."

Madame's voice stopped, and her eyes came back from looking somewhere through and beyond and focused again on me. "Dion," she said in a more normal tone, "perhaps you have heard that there are per-

sons with unusual psychic powers that enable them to establish contact with beings in other forms of existence. I am such a person, and I am responsible for what has happened at Alcott-Simpson's. But I want you to understand that I meant no evil. There should be no danger to anyone, and there *is* no danger to those whose experiences are limited in the usual way by their imperfect senses. But there can be danger to the individual whose experience is broadened too suddenly and too far. The danger is to the one who becomes involved beyond barriers he is not meant to cross. There are thresholds, Dion, that are meant to be crossed by the patient crawl of discipline and dedication, and to cross them by any short cut, even the short cut of love, can bring great danger." Madame stood up suddenly and motioned for me to do the same. "I know you are greatly confused and you have many questions. But I cannot say more. If you think carefully about what I have said, you will experience the truth more completely than if I tried to make you understand with many narrow words. It is only necessary that you remember that danger exists for you now at Alcott-Simpson's." .

Chapter 13

I RAN. I RAN ALL THE WAY HOME AND WENT RIGHT TO my room. Dad was out somewhere. He'd left some dinner for me on the stove but I didn't feel much like eating. I must have stayed in my room for about an hour, going over everything in my mind and deciding what to do.

In a way, the things I'd learned at Madame Stregovitch's hadn't shocked me as much as you might expect. Perhaps I'd already known some of it before in a wordless part of my mind. And it was almost a relief to have it put into words so that I could take it out and face it.

Part of it was very clear. Madame Stregovitch had made it possible for whomever or whatever it was—the ones Sara called the Others and Myrna called They—to invade Alcott-Simpson's. Some of the rest of it was harder to understand. Somehow a person in-between was needed to do what Madame had done, a person who was in between childhood and maturity. I was pretty sure that Sara had been that person.

There was one other thing that I didn't understand completely, though I got it enough to make me feel scared to death every time I thought about it. These invaders—these Others—were not dangerous *except* to someone who had become too closely involved with them. And that Sara was terribly involved was only too clear.

First, there was the fact that she was almost certainly the inbetween person Madame had used to summon them. And besides, even though I'd tried to fool myself with my "store executive's daughter" theory, it was pretty plain that without the help of the Others, Sara could not have known all the things she knew or done all the things she did. The Others had been protecting Sara from the guards and dogs, helping her to open doors and unlock locks, and maybe even telling her when I was looking for her. And in exchange what? What kind of hold over Sara's life had They taken in exchange?

I was sure that the things I had told Madame had made her realize how much danger Sara was in, and I knew that she was going to do whatever she could to help. But it worried me that Madame had said she might need my help at Alcott-Simpson's in a few days. It sounded as if she wasn't sure she could help Sara by herself. And I thought perhaps I knew why. It occurred to me that maybe Madame was afraid she was too late. That the Others would not let her find Sara and warn her. The last few times I had looked for Sara, I hadn't been able to find her. Maybe the Others had already hidden her or taken her away.

I knew that Madame meant well in telling me to stay away. I'd been kind of a pet of Madame's for years and years. It was natural that she wouldn't want me to get involved, too. What she didn't know was that in a way I already was involved. She didn't know how I felt about Sara. And how Sara felt about me, too—I was pretty sure of that. And that was why I felt that if she could still be helped—if she would really try to break away for anyone, maybe it would be for me. That was the reason I decided I couldn't obey Madame's warning and stay away.

The next day I didn't go to school. I went to my morning jobs because I had nothing else to do with the time; but as soon as Alcott-Simpson's opened for the day, I went inside. I went over the entire store, except for the area near the cosmetic counter. I got close enough once or twice to catch a glimpse of Madame, but I was very careful not to let her see me. It was all wasted effort, though. Sara just wasn't there.

Everything inside the store was pretty much the way it had been the day before. There were very few customers and fewer clerks than usual. Most of the clerks who were there were new, people I'd never seen before. The only real difference was that the toy department had been roped off, just as Madame had said it would be. After I had looked all the way through the store, I went out and wandered around town. In an hour or so I came back and looked again. And that's the way I spent the whole day. By closing time I knew what I had to do.

A few minutes after five o'clock, I went up to the sixth floor. I had noticed that there seemed to be only two clerks on the whole huge floor, so what I had in mind would not be hard to do. There was a scattering of customers, and I walked around looking at people as if I were looking for someone. When a clerk came up to me and asked me what I wanted, I said my mother was shopping somewhere in the store and I thought maybe she'd come up there. He left me alone then, and I wandered around until I saw my chance. I slipped into the same display room I had hidden in before and slid back under the same bed.

I lay there for what seemed a very long time, listening to the distant voices of the clerks and customers. Then the closing bell rang and almost immediately all the voices stopped. The clerks must have gone downstairs almost on the heels of the last customer. Apparently they didn't want to be left alone way up there on the sixth floor when the elevators stopped running and the lights went down.

I waited, lying there in the dust under the low bed. After a while the big lights went off and the silence widened around me. I waited a while longer to be sure that all the clerks had had time to leave the store. Then, just as the silence seemed complete, the other noises began.

They were the same noises I had heard before. There were faint whispering voices and muffled footsteps, always so soft and indistinct I could never quite rule out the possibility that perhaps I was imagining it all. I had been planning to climb out from under the bed and start looking for Sara as soon as I was sure the clerks had all gone home, but the noises kept me where I was. Somehow I felt I had to stay there until I could decide if I was really hearing something or not, as if deciding what I had to face when I came out would make it easier to face it.

But the noises went on and on, and I went on lying there, getting stiffer and stiffer from fright and from not moving, until I wondered if I would ever be able to get out at all. And then suddenly I heard someone saying my name. "Dion," the voice said, and there was a pause and everything was very quiet. The noises were all gone. "Dion, I'm here. Please come out."

It was Sara. I struggled out from under the bed and there she was, standing in the edge of the shadow on the other side of the room. I sat down on the side of the bed because my knees felt unhinged and my voice wouldn't start working. As soon as I could, I said, "Am I ever glad to see you."

Sara looked down and away so I couldn't see her eyes. "I'm glad to see you, too," she said. She was wearing a long dress again, but this one was pale blue with a scarf that was attached to one shoulder and went up over her head. "You shouldn't be here. You shouldn't have come, but I'm glad you're here."

I was so relieved to see her looking just the same as ever, as if nothing was really wrong, that for a second I almost forgot what I'd come to do. But then I remembered. "Sara, I've got to tell you something," I said, "but not here. Could we go somewhere else?"

"Somewhere else?" she asked. "What do you mean?"

"I mean outside. Could we get downstairs and outside without—I mean would you come some place outside the store with me?"

She stared at me, and her fantastic eyes seemed to get wider and wider and she made a sound like a gasp. "No, no I can't." She stepped back away from me as if she meant to turn and run.

"All right," I said quickly. "All right. Not outside. But isn't there a better place we could go—to talk. A better place than *this*." I rolled my eyes in a way that I hoped would tell her what I really meant.

"The garden?" Sara asked. "We could go down to the garden."

I started to say all right, but then I remembered how dark it would be there at night. And I remembered too about the boat that sailed by itself in the fountain. "No," I said, "not there."

"Wait, I know," Sara said. "We could go up on the roof. Have you ever been up on the roof?"

I said I never had, and I thought about it quickly and it seemed like a good idea. At least on the roof it would be wide open and you could know what was around you. It would be almost like being outside Alcott-Simpson's. Perhaps it *would* be like being outside Alcott-Simpson's, I thought—deliberately *not* thinking that perhaps They couldn't follow us there, as if I were afraid even to think what I really meant because the feeling was so strong that They were all around us, listening and watching. I nodded, "All right, let's go up on the roof."

Sara led the way to the emergency staircase, and we took the upward flight, up past the seventh floor where all the big offices were, to a little room that opened out onto the huge dark stretch of the open roof. To the West the horizon still glowed with sunset, and far to the East the sky was a clear blue-black, sparkling with stars, but the fog had settled again on the center of town and it was very dark. All around us the fog blotted out the edges of the roof so that it seemed endless, as if we were walking through dark clouds on a tar-paper and gravel infinity.

We walked for a way without talking. A slow damp wind lifted Sara's hair and the pale blue scarf, and mixed them with the mist that closed in like a wave behind our backs. Finally a low wall with a wide ledge took shape just ahead. We came to an edge of the roof and looked over. The lights of Palm Ave, blurred and hazy, shone up from what seemed much more than seven stories down below. We leaned on the ledge and looked down into the fog flooded canyon.

"Sara," I began, "since I saw you last, I've found out some very important things."

Sara turned towards me, and the scarf fell across her face leaving only her eyes unveiled. "Yes," she agreed, "I thought you had."

"I found out all about the ones you call the Others," I said. "I know all about it now—who They are and how They came here to Alcott-Simpson's."

She nodded sadly. "I didn't want you to find out," she said. "I tried to make them stay away from you. I was afraid you wouldn't like me any more if you found out. But They wouldn't remember."

"It doesn't matter. It doesn't change how I feel about you," I said. "It's not your fault."

"Yes, it's my fault. I shouldn't ever have come here. It wasn't right for me. And it isn't right for you."

"Well, maybe," I said, "but anyway—" I stopped and looked around, but nothing moved except the fog and there was no sound except the distant fog-muffled drone of the city. "Anyway it will all be over soon. They, the Others, are going to have to go away soon."

"I know," Sara said, "I am going to have to go away, too. I'll have to go with Them—"

"No!" I said, and it came out almost a shout. "You mustn't let Them make you think that. You don't belong with Them. They only want to make you think you do. You're going to come away right now with me. You just have to make up your mind that you are going with me no matter what. We'll go down the stairs very quickly, and if They lock the doors, we'll go down the escalator; and if you see Them or hear Them don't slow down, and we'll—"

I stopped. The wind had come up suddenly, and the air swirling around us was so heavy with white mist that Sara's dress and hair blended into the twisting fingers of fog. But I could still see her face clearly. She moved closer to me, and her eyes were shining with a kind of wild excitement. "Do you want to come with me, Dion?" she said, and her voice was strange, too high and light.

"Yes," I said. "Yes," and suddenly a wave of terrible excitement broke inside my mind. A part of me struggled and then drowned, and then the fog was full of small soft hands pushing me, and I moved with them willingly towards the edge. But when I looked down, far down to the dark street, a last stab of fear broke through the numb willingness. The fear of falling was a sharp pain in the backs of my legs, and I felt my face twist with terror.

"No," Sara said, and suddenly she was between me and the edge of the roof. The wild brightness was gone from her face, and her eyes were soft and steady and very sad. "I'm sorry," she said, but I only stared at her without saying anything, because suddenly I knew—and there was nothing to say.

"I'm sorry," she said again. "It's my fault. I shouldn't have let you come here. I shouldn't ever have let you see me." She was moving back, away from

me into the fog. "I should never have come here at all. Only the very little ones were sent for, but some of them were my brothers and sisters and so I came, too. But I was too old just to play—and then I saw you——"

The fog came down then and closed in between us, but in a moment I heard her voice calling, "Dion, Dion, this way." I followed the sound, and it led to the little shed where the emergency stairway came out onto the roof. Sara was not there. I wound my way down the stairs for what seemed like miles and miles. My mind felt numb, and my legs were so weak and shaky that sometimes I thought I would have to stop. When I finally got to the ground floor and started down the Mall to the east entrance, the numbness had gotten worse so that I felt I was fighting to stay conscious. I wasn't sure I could make it through the doors to the outside. Then, just as I was almost there, I heard someone call my name. It was Madame Stregovitch, coming towards me down the Mall. I didn't even wonder why she was there. I only remember her catching me by the arms and the fierce burning of her eyes. Then I began to slip down and down into a soft and sleepy darkness.

When I woke up, I was lying on the bench in the alcove behind Ladies Gloves. No one else was there. If Madame Stregovitch had really been in Alcott-Simpson's, she had gone off and left me there alone. I rushed to the east entrance in a panic. The door was unlocked, and I burst out into a clear, dark night.

Chapter 14

THE NEXT FEW DAYS HAVE FADED IN MY MIND. IT'S strange because I've always had such a good memory. But those days, right after that last night at Alcott-Simpson's, are all jumbled up in a haze of events and feelings and fears. There are a few things that stand out clear and sharp, but I'm not sure about sequence and things like that.

I know I stayed out of school two more days that week. I hardly ever miss school so of course Dad wanted to know what the matter was. I guess it was the first day I stayed home that I ran into Dad in the kitchen about nine o'clock.

"Dion," he said. "What are you doing at home? Are you sick?"

"No" I said. "I just overslept. I had some trouble getting to sleep last night, and when I finally did, I guess I just overslept."

Dad looked worried. I'd been getting myself off in the mornings since I was a little kid, and I was never late. Of course, I didn't always go to school because of the operations; but if I was going at all, I got there on time. Dad put some coffee on to perk and fixed himself some cereal before he said anything more, but after he sat down at the table he said, "Well, then, why don't you take advantage of the opportunity and get a rest? You look tired. You know I've told you I think you're on much too strenuous a schedule. I have some home lessons this morning so the place should be fairly quiet for a while. Why don't you go back to bed and really catch up on your sleep?"

I shrugged. "I might. I don't much like to go into class late." So I stayed home that day and the next, not doing much except thinking. Dad asked questions once or twice, but he didn't pressure me to get back to school.

The second day I went back to Alcott-Simpson's, feeling very sure I'd find everything just the way it had always been. At that particular point I'd almost convinced myself that I'd had some kind of complicated nightmare, and that everything would be back to normal. But instead I found the store closed and locked and huge sheets of paper pasted over all the windows. I came home in a kind of panic.

Back at our house I picked up the morning paper and it was full of stuff about the sudden, startling failure of the fabulous Alcott-Simpson department store. The articles went on and on about the history of Alcott-Simpson's—how it had for so many years been almost a symbol of a way of life—and how it had stood for a kind of service and a standard of quality that were fast becoming unknown—and that its passing was a great loss to the discerning and particular shopper. There was another article about why the store had closed.

The story started CHANGING TIMES FORCE END OF GREAT STORE. It was full of quotes from the managers. They explained the whole thing by saying that Alcott-Simpson's was built on a lavish scale at a time when such things were more widely appreciated, and that in these modern times it was too difficult to maintain. This fact, plus the growing competition from suburban shopping centers, had finally become decisive. The article went on like that, quoting more or less the same thing said in slightly different ways by different owners and managers. I read it over three times. Someone did mention that there had also been an increase in the usual problems with thieves and vandals, but that was the closest any of them came to saying anything much at all.

It was the end of the week when I decided to go back to Madame Stregovitch's house. When I got there it looked at first as if there was no one at home. I knocked on the door several times without getting an answer, and when I peeked in through the little oval window it looked very dark and empty. Finally, just as I was about to give up and go away, I heard something moving and a light came on.

I had a definite shock when Madame opened the door. For a minute I almost didn't recognize her. She was wearing a long robe-like thing, and her black and silver hair, that I'd always seen piled up on top of her head, was hanging down her back. She looked tired, and there were dark shadows around her eyes.

"Hey, are you sick again or something?" I said. "I'm sorry I bothered you."

"No, no. Come in. I'm very glad you came," Madame said, and as soon as she began to talk, she seemed more like herself. "If you had not come soon I would have sent for you. I wanted to see you before I left."

"Before you left?" I said. "Are you going away?"

"Yes," she said. "Very soon."

"I'm sorry," I said. "I'll miss you. I guess you lost your job when the store closed. Have you found another job somewhere else?"

Madame nodded. "Yes. I have found other work to do. But I wanted very much to see you before I left. I wished to tell you good-by—and also, there are some explanations I feel I must make."

When she said that about explanations, I felt a kind of weight lift in my mind. "That's what I need," I said, "explanations! You know, the last few days have been pretty bad." I gave a little laugh so neither of us would take it too seriously, but I think I really meant it. "Sometimes I've been pretty sure I must be cracking up."

Madame frowned. "You must not think that. Hasn't it occurred to you that you are not alone in your affliction? Doesn't it seem strange to you that so many others at Alcott-Simpson's have at the same time become also insane?"

"Look," I said, "I don't know what happened to other people at Alcott-Simpson's. Sure, they had to shut it down, but you saw what the papers said about the reasons. I don't know what the real reasons were."

"The *real* reasons," Madame said slowly. "*Reality*. It is a strange word. Everyone supposes that they know its meaning, but in truth it has meant different things to every age and to every individual. What has been real today may, in the future, become only a dream, and things beyond belief may become tomorrow's realities."

I guess it was plain that I wasn't getting any less confused, because all at once Madame stopped and held up her hand. "Yes, yes, you must have a more direct answer. You will not understand fully, but I feel that I owe you at least such explanation as I can give."

"You owe me?" I asked.

"Yes," she said, "I owe you an explanation because I am to some extent responsible for your confusion." Madame's lips twitched with a flicker of her usual biting humor. "You see, I do not claim full responsibility, because I feel certain something of the sort would have had to happen, sooner or later. Those who accept without question so incredible a world as Alcott-Simpson's, must not expect to ignore forever other worlds no more incredible. But enough of that—as I said, you cannot hope to understand fully, but I can perhaps help you to see that it is not your sanity that has been at fault."

Madame paused as if she were collecting her thoughts, and then she suddenly pointed to the picture on the mantle, the one with the strange magnetic eyes. "You noticed, the other day, the picture of my mother?" I nodded. "Many years ago my mother was known in many countries as a person of unusual powers, psychic powers. When I was a young child, the country in which we were living fell under the control of evil leaders, and because my mother spoke freely of the events she was able to foresee—of the suffering these leaders would cause and the terrible fate that would finally be theirs—she was taken away. I managed to escape, and I lived in hiding for many years in several countries. Then, when I was almost a woman, I began to discover that I had to some extent inherited the gifts that had been my mother's. But like many young ones, I chose another way. I did not want the life, and the death, that had been my mother's. I was at an age when other forces, normal forces, are very strong, so I ran away. I finally arrived in this country, and I worked and lived in many ways and in many places. At last I came to Alcott-Simpson's, and there, as you know, I have been for many years."

I leaned forward and opened my mouth, but Ma-

157

dame held up her hand and went on. "Why did I stay in such a place?" I gulped because it was exactly what I was going to ask. "I stayed because, after all those years, I was still running away and I felt safer there. Better than in most places, I was able there to shut out knowledge that I did not want, contacts that I wished not to make. Alcott-Simpson's shuts out many things."

I nodded. "I've always had a feeling like that about it. Like it was a separate world."

"Exactly. And it was so for me until not long ago. Then one day I happened to see an article about some gifts in that special world—some very special and unusual gifts. And on the next page I read about what seemed, indeed, to be a very different world. It was a story about children in a country where for some years now there has been much famine."

All of a sudden I knew what she was talking about. "I remember," I said. "You gave me part of that magazine for my scrapbook. And I remember something strange about it. It was some eyes. Some eyes that came right through when you held it up to the light. Did you notice that?"

Madame's eyes whipped up at me so sharply that I jumped as if I'd been hit. "Indeed I did notice," she said. "Those eyes, those strangely misplaced eyes, were what gave me the inspiration to do what I did. For many years I had tried to forget things I was afraid to know, but such knowledge is not easily forgotten.

Among the things I remembered was the means used to send a particular invitation to a very special kind of visitor. Only one thing was lacking. In order for me to accomplish what I had decided to do, I needed the unknowing cooperation of an adolescent—the mind of a sleeping or unconscious child. Then one day as I walked through Alcott-Simpson's, there on a bench in an alcove was the missing ingredient."

"M-m-me?" I stammered in absolute amazement.

Madame nodded. "I am afraid that you are right. It was you. But you must believe that I did not anticipate that your involvement would be any more than the momentary use I put you to. I did not foresee the danger to which you would be exposed. I still do not understand why it happened."

"I think I know," I said. "It was only because of—of Sara." It hurt to say her name, and even to think about her brought a dull undimming pain. "She told me why she came—and why she shouldn't have. She said the Others were all younger. I guess they were happy enough with all the things to play with, but Sara was too old for just that."

I sat for a while staring at my hands. "And now—are they gone?" I asked. "Are they *all* gone?"

Madame nodded. "On that last day I, too, hid myself and stayed after closing in the store. I knew I dared wait no longer. I planned to try to send them back by other means; but as I had feared, it was not possible. Then once again, my missing ingredient appeared, just when he was needed—entirely against orders, but I must admit, most opportunely." Madame smiled, and I could tell she was trying to sound cheerful to make me feel better.

I tried. "That's me," I said, "always handy." But it didn't come off. I couldn't hide how I really felt.

"I'm sorry," Madame said, and I'd never heard her sound so gentle. "You must think of it as a sad but beautiful mystery. It is, indeed, a mystery—so complete a materialization. Such a thing is very rare. But then her reason was very strong—the strongest reason of all, for love in itself is the greatest of mysteries."

That was all. We sat there a little longer without saying anything, and then I got up to go. At the door Madame said, "Dion, I must tell you again that I am sorry. Very sorry for what I have done to you, and even a little sorry for the mischief I have done to Alcott-Simpson's."

It seemed to me that that was a strange way to put it. As far as I could see, "mischief" didn't begin to cover it. "Mischief?" I said.

Madame shrugged, and the corner of her mouth twitched in something like a smile. "Call it what you will. I meant it only as mischief. Had I meant something more, I could have opened the doors to very different visitors. I might have lowered a drawbridge to powerful and evil invaders. But instead, one could say, perhaps, that I only unlatched the back gate for the neighbor's children."

That was the way it ended.

I thought it through to the very end, and then I wrote the last verse. It goes like this:

The police are baffled, the management's frantic,
The watchmen will not stay.
All the scientific investigators,
Gave up and went away,
And they all pretend that they can't be certain,
For nobody wants to say
That the ghosts,
Little ghosts
Who lost their childhood,
Have been sent to Alcott's to play.

Chapter 15

IT HAS BEEN ABOUT SIX MONTHS NOW SINCE ALCOTT-Simpson's closed and Madame Stregovitch went away. Looking at just the outside of things, you might say that nothing has changed very much; but from another point of view everything is entirely different.

We still live in the same old place, and I still go to Randolph High School. The main difference at Randolph is A-Group. That's what we call the folk-rock band that Jerry and Brett and I have formed with another guy named Johnson on the drums. We've really been doing all right. We've played for a lot of school dances, and we've even had a few outside jobs for money. I've been writing music again lately, and a lot of my stuff we do in the group. But an even more startling development is that Brett and I do most of the singing. If anyone had told me a year ago that I'd be singing in front of several hundred people—particularly several hundred high school kids—I'd have told them they were crazy. But it wasn't so hard after the first few times. I guess I do all right.

I don't mean by that that I've turned into any big personality sensation or anything like that. As a matter of fact, except for the guys in the band, I still don't have any gang that I really belong to. But there are two or three bunches of kids that I see a little of now and then. The funny thing is I've found out that that's the way I like it. I have some friends here and there, and I don't have to get hung up on anybody else's action. I don't know how the whole thing happened, except that when I forgot to keep up the big social effort I'd been making ever since I came to Randolph, I just slid back into my own style; and the surprising part was that it was all right. It's not flashy, but it's comfortable and it comes out of what I am, instead of something I have to keep spreading around on top.

At home things look almost the same on the outside, too. My Dad still drifts along with pretty much the same bunch of students, not to mention the same little army of friends and acquaintances. He did have a spell of trying to make some changes a few months back, but nothing much came of it. It was pretty much to be expected—at his age and right here in the same old environment. But when I get fed up, and I still do now and then, I have to remember that I have only myself to blame. I had a chance to change things, and I didn't take it.

I had the chance a few months ago right after Alcott-Simpson's closed down. It happened at dinner one night towards the end of that week when I stayed home from school and just sat around thinking and worrying. I remember that Dad had made my favorite kind of stew, and while we were eating all of a sudden he said, "Di, I've been thinking about something, and I believe I've come to a decision. I was talking to John again yesterday and apparently that job in the music department at Wentworth still hasn't been filled. How would it be if I called up to see if I could arrange an appointment? Then you and I could get all slicked up and make a trip out there tomorrow to see if we can convince Mr. Marple that we would be worthy members of the Wentworth family."

Dad's friend John, who teaches at Wentworth, is always talking about this Marple guy. He is the principal at Wentworth, but he likes to call himself the "Headmaster," and he is always talking about the "Wentworth Family." John says Marple has a Father-Figure complex with a capital F; and if he's heard of academic freedom, he thinks it means letting his staff go home at night instead of locking them in the storeroom with the other school property. He's very big on things like "professional appearance" and being seen at the right places and *not* at any of the wrong ones.

All of a sudden I got a mental picture of scruffy old Dad with his hair slicked back, trying to put on some kind of an act for this Marple character. I didn't say anything for quite a while, and at last Dad said, "Di?"

"Well, go ahead if you want to," I said, "but as

far as I'm concerned I'd rather stay right here. Seems to me that for someone who's used to city life, the suburbs would be a real drag."

I got up then and put my dishes in the sink, and as I left the kitchen I got a glimpse of Dad's face. If you could have framed his expression, you would have had to label it, "The Last Minute Reprieve."

To tell the truth, what I did then—I mean turning down a chance to move—wasn't just pure heart on my part. Happening right at that particular moment, my mind was so crowded and confused that I didn't want to face any other big new change right then. But later on, when I'd had time to consider it, I began to get some ideas about what Dad's offer really represented, I mean for a guy like him. He might as well have volunteered for a stretch in Sing Sing. And then, after a while, when things began to change a little at Randolph and we got A-Group under way, I began to lose interest in changing schools anyway.

Like I say, I still get fed up at times, but in the last few months the trouble between my dad and me has begun to ease up a little. I've been doing some reading and thinking about the subject of rebellion, and it seems to me that the whole thing was probably inevitable. It seems to me that rebellion is usually inevitable, and that it only gets useless when you forget that it's just a doorway and not a destination. Because if you settle down in a doorway, your future is going to be pretty narrow.

And speaking of destinations—mine is a lot more up in the air than it used to be. I have at least half a dozen plans that I'm fooling around with. I can't seem to make up my mind. It's kind of funny actually, when I used to be so sure of what I wanted—all those years when I was planning to be an executive at Alcott-Simpson's someday. And now I have to start planning all over again. But I don't mind. There are a lot of things I'm interested in, and planning is still something that I like to do.

Just a few days ago they started tearing Alcott-Simpson's down. I guess they're going to build a huge new office building on the spot. I went by one day to watch, but I didn't stay long. I didn't like the way it made me feel. I don't mind thinking about the things that happened at the store last spring, but I didn't like thinking about it *there*, with the wrecking ball crashing into the walls. Last night, for instance, when I got the idea for the song, I started thinking about all of it, and I thought it through from beginning to end; and it didn't bother me at all. For one thing, I've quit worrying about what I believe.

I don't know what other people believe happened to Alcott-Simpson's, and maybe I don't even know for sure what I believe. But what *happened* to me was real, and Sara was real, and the difference in me is as real as the difference there'll be in Alcott-Simpson's when they've finished with that wrecking ball.

Now that I've thought about the song some more

The police are baffled the managment's
frantic. The watchmen will not stay
All the scientific   investigators
gave up and   went away.
And they all pr   pretend that
they can't be   certain for
nobody   wants to say
that   the ghosts, little
ghosts who lost
their childhood
Have
been
sent to
Alcott's to play.

—the Fishbowl Song—I don't think I'll show it to Brett and Jerry after all. It's a good song, but it wouldn't mean too much to them, or maybe to anyone else but me. Instead I guess I'll put it away in a box of important things I keep in my bottom desk drawer. I'll put it in my scrapbook with the magazine articles that Madame Stregovitch gave me—the ones with the fishbowl and the eyes.

The two articles have been there since right after Madame Stregovitch went away. That was when I took them out of the scrapbook and put them in the drawer where I could get them out and look at them now and then. Every time I do, it amazes me how I was able to look at them that first time and not have it tell me anything. Oh, I noticed the eyes, all right, looking out through the fur lining of the fishbowl—but it didn't mean a thing to me except an interesting accidental effect. And that just goes to show you how stupid a human being can be.

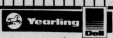